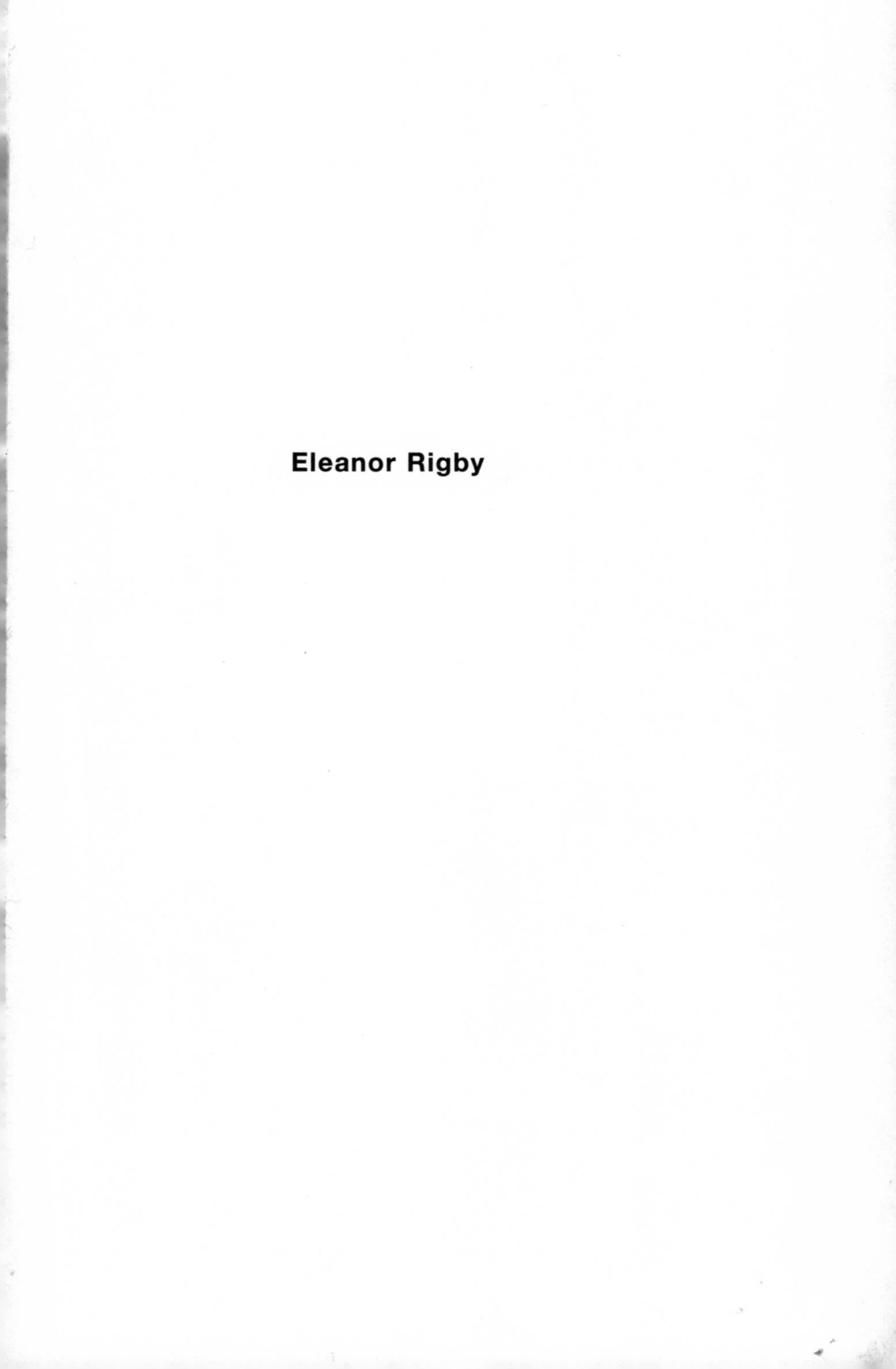

Eleanor Rigby

By the Same Author

Fiction:

Generation X

Shampoo Planet

Life After God

Microserfs

Girlfriend in a Coma

Miss Wyoming

All Families Are Psychotic

Hey Nostradamus!

Nonfiction:

Polaroids from the Dead

City of Glass

Souvenir of Canada

Souvenir of Canada 2

Eleanor Rigby

A Novel

Douglas Coupland

BLOOMSBURY

For information address Bloomsbury Publishing, 175 Fifth Avenue, New York, NY 10010.

Published by Bloomsbury Publishing, New York and London
Distributed to the trade by Holtzbrinck Publishers

All papers used by Bloomsbury Publishing are natural, recyclable products made from wood grown in well-managed forests. The manufacturing processes conform to the environmental regulations of the country of origin.

Library of Congress Cataloging-in-Publication Data has been applied for.

ISBN 1-58234-523-6
ISBN-13 9781582345239

First U.S. Edition 2005

10 9 8 7 6 5 4 3 2 1

Printed in the United States of America
by Quebecor World Fairfield

I had always thought that a person born blind and given sight later on in life through the miracles of modern medicine would feel reborn. Just imagine looking at our world with brand new eyes, everything fresh, covered with dew and charged with beauty—pale skin and yellow daffodils, boiled lobsters and a full moon. And yet I've read books that tell me this isn't the way newly created vision plays out in real life. Gifted with sight, previously blind patients become frightened and confused. They can't make sense of shape or colour or depth. Everything shocks, and nothing brings solace. My brother, William, says, "Well think about it, Liz—kids lie in their cribs for nearly a year watching hand puppets and colourful toys come and go. They're dumb as planks, and it takes them a long time to even twig to the notion of where they end and the world begins. Why should it be any different just because you're older and technically wiser?"

In the end, those gifted with new eyesight tend to retreat into their own worlds. Some beg to be made blind again, yet when they consider it further, they hesitate, and realize they're unable to surrender their sight. Bad visions are better than no visions.

Here's something else I think about: in the movies, the way criminals are ready to squeal so long as they're entered into a witness relocation program. They're given a brand new name, passport and home, but they'll never be able to contact anybody from their old life again; they have to choose between death and becoming someone entirely new. But you know what I think? I think the FBI simply shoots everybody who enters the program. The fact that nobody ever hears from these dead participants perversely convinces outsiders that the program really works. Let's face it: they go to the same magic place in the country where people take their unwanted pets.

Listen to me go on like this. My sister, Leslie, says I'm morbid, but I don't agree. I think I'm reasonable, just trying to be honest with myself about the ways of the world. Or come up with new ways of seeing them. I once read that for every person currently alive on earth, there are nineteen dead people who have lived before us. That's not that much really. Our existence as a species on earth has been so short. We forget that.

I sometimes wonder how big a clump you could make if you were to take all creatures that have ever lived—not just people, but giraffes, plankton, amoebas, ferns and dinosaurs—and smush them all together in a big ball, a planet. The gravitational mass of this new clump would make it implode into a tiny ball as hot as the sun's surface. Steam would sizzle out into space. But just *maybe* the iron in the blood of all of these creatures would be too heavy to leap out into space, and *maybe* a small and angry little planet with a molten iron core would form. And just *maybe,* on that new planet, life would start all over again.

I mention all of this because of the comet that passed earth seven years ago, back in 1997—Hale-Bopp, a chunk of some other demolished planet hurtling about the universe. I first saw it just past sunset while standing in the parking lot of Rogers Video. Teenage cliques dressed like hooligans and sluts were pointing up, at this small dab of slightly melted butter in the blue-black heavens above Hollyburn Mountain. Sure, I think the zodiac is pure hooey, but when an entirely new object appears in the sky, it opens some kind of window to your soul and to your sense of destiny. No matter how rational you try to be, it's hard to escape the feeling that such a celestial event portends some kind of radical change.

Funny that it took a comet to trigger a small but radical change in my life. In the years until then, I'd been sieving the contents of my days with ever finer mesh, trying to sort out those sharp and nasty bits that were causing me grief: bad ideas, pointless habits, robotic thinking. Like anybody, I wanted to find out if my life was ever going to make sense, or maybe even feel like a story. In the wake of Hale-Bopp, I realized that my life, while technically adequate, had become all it was ever going to be. If I could just keep things going on their current even keel for a few more decades, the coroner could dump me into a peat bog without my ever having once gone fully crazy.

I made the radical change standing in the video store's parking lot, holding copies of *On the Beach, Bambi, Terms of Endearment, How Green Was My Valley* and *The Garden of the Finzi-Continis,* staring up at the comet. I decided that instead of demanding certainty from life, I now wanted peace. No more trying to control everything—it was now time to go with the flow. With that one decision, the chain-mail shroud I'd been wearing my entire life fell from my body and I was light as a gull. I'd freed myself.

* * *

Of course, we're born alone, and when we die, we join every living thing that's ever existed—and ever will. When I'm dead I won't be lonely any more—I'll be joining a big party. Sometimes at the office, when the phones aren't ringing, and when I've completed my daily paperwork, and when The Dwarf To Whom I Report is still out for lunch, I sit in my chest-high sage green cubicle and take comfort in knowing that since I don't remember where I was before I was born, why should I be worried about where I go after I die?

In any event, were you to enter the cubicle farm that is Landover Communication Systems, you probably wouldn't notice me, daydreaming or otherwise. I long ago learned to render myself invisible. I pull myself into myself, and my eyes become stale and dull. One of my favourite things on TV is when an actor is in a casket pretending to be dead, or, even more challenging, laid out on a morgue's steel draining pan bathed in clinical white light. *Did I see an eyelash flicker? Did that cheek muscle just twitch? Is the thorax pumping slightly?* Is this particular fascination of mine goofy, or is it sick?

I'm alone now, and I was alone when I saw my first comet that night in the parking lot, the comet that lightened my burden in life. It made me so giddy, I chucked the rented tapes into my Honda's back seat and went for a walk over to Ambleside Beach. For once I didn't look wistfully at all the couples and parents and families headed back to their cars, or at the teenagers arriving to drink and drug and screw all night in between the logs on the sand.

A comet!

The sky!

Me!

The moon was full and glamorous—so bright it made me want to do a crossword puzzle under its light, just to see if I could. I took off my runners and, with them in hand, I walked into the seafoam and looked west, out at Vancouver Island and the Pacific. I remembered an old Road Runner versus Coyote cartoon—one in which the Coyote buys the world's most powerful magnet. When he turns it on, hundreds of astonishing things come flying across the desert toward him: tin cans, keys, grand pianos, money and weapons. I felt like I'd just activated a similar sort of magnet, and I needed to wait and see what came flying across the oceans and deserts to meet me.

* * *

My name is Liz Dunn. I've never been married, I'm right-handed and my hair is deep red and wilfully curly. I may or may not snore—there's never been anybody to tell me one way or the other. There was a reason I'd rented such weepy movies on the night I first saw Hale-Bopp. The next morning I was scheduled to have my two lower wisdom teeth removed—two big popcorn-shaped suckers that decided late in life to turn sideways and attack my molars.

I was thirty-six, for Pete's sake. I'd booked off the following week and was preparing myself accordingly: Jell-O and tinned food and broth soups. The videos were part of a *verklempt*-o-thon movie festival I planned to hold for myself. If painkillers were going to make me mushy, best to take control of the situation. I wanted to blubber shamelessly, and do so for seven straight days.

The next morning, Mother gave me a ride to the dental surgery clinic down on Fell Avenue, and although her life was as empty as mine, she made it seem as if I'd just made her reschedule her Nobel Prize acceptance ceremony in order to drive me. "You know, I was supposed to have lunch with Sylvia today. The portable kennel she bought for Empress broke in the first five minutes, and the woman is so weak-willed I have to go into Petcetera when she takes it back and be her bad cop."

"Mother, I'd have taken a cab if it was allowed, but it has to be a family member or friend to pick you up. You know that."

It was decades past the point where Mother chided me for my lack of friends. She said, "Empress is a lovely dog."

"Really?" Empress, from my experience, was a shrill, yappy, neurotic varmint.

"You should get a dog, Elizabeth."

"I'm allergic, Mother."

"What about a hypoallergenic breed, a poodle?"

"The hypoallergenic thing is a folk tale."

"It is?"

"It is. You can minimize reactions, but that's all. And it's not the fur that's the issue. It's the dander, saliva and urine on top of the fur."

"Pardon me for trying to help you out."

"I looked into pets long ago, Mother. Trust me."

Our arrival at the clinic put a quick end to that conversation. It was an eight-storey building from the sixties—one of those buildings I've driven by a thousand times and never noticed, sort of like the architectural version of myself. Inside, it was cool and smelled of sanitation products. The print on the elevator's DOOR CLOSE button was almost worn off. I pointed it out to Mother and said, "I bet there are a few psychiatrists in this building."

"What makes you say that?"

"Look at the button."

"So?"

"In the elevator industry, a DOOR CLOSE button is called a pacifier button. They're installed simply to give the illusion of control to your elevator ride. They're almost never hooked up to a real switch."

"I still think you should get a dog."

I have to admit that I love hospitals, clinics and medical environments. You enter them, you sit in a chair and suddenly all the burden of having to remain alive just floats away—that endless brain-churning buzzing and second-guessing and non-stop short-term planning that accompanies the typical lonely life.

I'd never met the day's exodontist before, a hearty Australian who rustled up jokes and cheer even for my sad little face under its laughing gas mask.

"So where'd you go to school then, Lizzie?"

"Liz. Here in North Van—Carson Graham for high school."

"Ho ho! And after that?"

"Oh God. BCIT. Accounting."

"Marvellous. Lots of partying there?"

"What?" The anaesthetist clamped the mask harder onto my face.

"You know. Letting loose. Getting down."

"My life is not a beer commercial . . ."

That's when I went under. A second later I opened my eyes and the room was empty save for a nurse putting away the last of a set of tools. My mouth felt packed with sand. I smiled because it had been such a great thing to be conked out like that—one moment you're dealing with an Australian comedian, the next you're . . . *gone.* One more reason to no longer fear death.

In the car on the way home, my conversation with Mother consisted mostly of her sighing and me mumbling like a faraway radio station. She dropped me off outside my condo, and before she raced off to Petcetera she said, "Really think about a dog now, Elizabeth."

"Let it *go,* Muddah."

It was a hot dry day. August. The building's entryway smelled of sun-roasted cedar-bark chips and underwatered junipers. Inside, it was cool, smelling instead of the lobby's decaying nylon rug. Once inside my place, three floors up, I had the eerie sensation that I was watching a movie version of a still room. There was nothing in it that moved or denoted time's passage—no plants or clocks—and I felt guilty to be wasting all of that invisible film, ashamed that my condo was so boring. But then again, the right kind of boring can be peaceful, and peace was my new perspective on the world. Just go with the flow.

My head throbbed and I went into my bedroom and laid it

down on a cool pillow. The pillow warmed up, I turned it over to the cool side and then I fell asleep. When I woke up it was past sunset, but in the sky up above the mountain there was still some light and colour. I cursed because an afternoon nap always leads to an endless night. I touched my face: both sides swollen like the mumps. I fell back onto the mattress and my tongue explored the two new salty, bloody socket holes and their thorny stitches.

* * *

The Liz Dunns of this world tend to get married, and then twenty-three months after their wedding and the birth of their first child they establish sensible, lower-maintenance hairdos that last them forever. Liz Dunns take classes in croissant baking, and would rather chew on soccer balls than deny their children muesli. They own one sex toy, plus one cowboy fantasy that accompanies its use. No, not a cowboy—more like a guy who builds decks—expensive designer decks with built-in multi-faucet spas—a guy who would take hours, if necessary, to help such a Liz find the right colour of grout for the guest-room tile reno.

I am a traitor to my name: I'm not cheerful or domestic. I'm drab, crabby and friendless. I fill my days fighting a constant battle to keep my dignity. Loneliness is my curse—our species' curse—it's the gun that shoots the bullets that make us dance on a saloon floor and humiliate ourselves in front of strangers.

Where does loneliness come from? I'd hazard a guess that the crapshoot that is family has more than a little to do with it—father's a drunk; mother's an agoraphobic; single child; middle child; firstborn; mother's a nag; father's a golf cheat . . . I mean, what's your own nature/nurture crapshoot? You're here. You're reading these words. Is this a coincidence? Maybe you think fate is only for others. Maybe you're ashamed to be reading about loneliness—maybe someone will catch you and then they'll know your secret stain. And then maybe you're not even very sure what loneliness is—that's common. We cripple our children for life by not telling them what loneliness is, all of its shades and tones and implications. When it clubs us on the head, usually just after we leave home, we're blindsided. We have no idea what hit us. We think we're diseased, schizoid, bipolar, monstrous and lacking in dietary chromium. It takes us until thirty to figure out what it was that sucked the joy from our youth, that made our brains shriek and burn on the inside, even while our exteriors made us seem as confident and bronzed as Qantas pilots. Loneliness.

* * *

The message on my answering machine the next morning was from The Dwarf To Whom I Report. His name is Liam.

> *I hope your surgery went okay, Liz. You didn't miss too much here at the office. I'm having Donna courier you over a few files for you to pick away at over the next week while you recover. Sorry I missed you. Call any time.*

What? I didn't miss anything? Heaven forbid anything even quasi-dramatic might occur in the cubicle farm of Landover Communication Systems . . .

Liz, there was a fire . . .

Liz, we all got naked at lunch hour and interfered with each other . . .

Liz, those voices in my head? They're real.

Well, the thing about Liam is that he actually *enjoys* his work. This is inconceivable to me. On a few occasions I've tried to mimic his cheer, but no go. To me a job is a job is a job, and before you know it, *poof!* it's all over and they're throwing your ashes off Lions Gate Bridge.

Liam feels many things I don't, for example a sense of mission as well as indifference to the emotional lives of others, including me. This is possibly to be expected, as I'm plain, unsalvageably plain. When I was born, the doctor took one look as he held me, bloodied and squalling, and asked the nurse if there was anything good on TV that night. My parents looked at me, said, "Well, whatever," and then discussed what colour to reupholster the living-room sofa. I'm only half joking.

People look at me and forget I'm here. To be honest, I don't even have to try to make myself invisible, it just happens. But evidently I'm not invisible enough to Liam, especially if he thought I might like to "pick away at a few files" while I get over these teeth.

* * *

One of my big problems is time sickness. When I feel lonely, I assume that the mood will never pass—that I'll feel lonely and bad for the rest of my life, which means that I've wrecked both the present and the future. And if I look back on my past, I wreck that too, by concentrating on all the things I did wrong. The brutal thing about time sickness is that naming it is no cure.

I look at the philodendron on the kitchen windowsill, the only thing in my condo that ever changes. I found it at a bus stop twelve years ago and I've kept it going ever since. I like it because up close its leaves are pretty, and also because it makes me think of time in a way that doesn't totally depress me.

If I could go back in time two decades and give just one piece of advice to a younger me, it would be, "Don't worry so damn much." But because young people never believe old people, I'd most likely ignore my own advice.

If there's a future Liz Dunn out there in, say, 2034, may I respectfully ask you to time travel back to right now and give me the advice I need? I promise you, I'll listen, and I'll give you a piece of my philodendron to take back with you so you can grow your own plant there.

* * *

I ended up sleeping until the next afternoon—surgery can really take a whack out of you. My *verklempt*-o-thon was well in progress when my older sister Leslie dropped by, intruding upon one of the most wrenching of my *verklempt*-o-thon's moments, the end of *The Garden of the Finzi-Continis* when the family realizes they're doomed to the gas chambers. I was slightly looped on Percocets, and my eyes were hound-dog red.

"You look like hell, Liz. Like you have mumps."

"Thank you, Leslie, but I can't say the same for you."

"It's this jacket—it's new. What do you think?" Leslie twirled on the carpet. Leslie's beauty truly makes me a genetic punchline. When we were young, no amount of documentation could convince us we were biological sisters.

"It's very you." *Cripes.* Leslie vomits and pieces of undigested *Vanity Fair* articles come up—but she's never fooled me for a moment with her fashion slave persona. I see through it, which is why she relaxes around me.

"Look at this place, Liz. Open the curtains."

"No."

"Okay then, I think I'll smoke."

"Sure." I like cigarette smoke in a room. At least then the room doesn't look or feel dead.

We lit up, and Leslie surveyed the condo with her real estate agent's eye for upsellability. *Sparkling Norgate Park fixer-upper/1bdr/1bth/character kitchen/one owner.* "Did Mother torture you yesterday?"

I paused the video. "She had to cancel lunch with Sylvia."

"Cancelling lunch with Sylvia? That's a baddy. Did it inch up the guilt a notch or two?"

"I . . . Don't get me started."

"I'd have driven you if it weren't for the kids' recital."

Leslie kept shrugging her shoulders in a hunched way I'd never before seen. "Leslie, you look fidgety, and what's with the shoulders?"

"My tits are killing me."

"Still?"

I thought she'd inhale the whole cigarette in one drag. "Good God, yes." The exhaled smoke resembled the Challenger explosion. "Oh, to be flat like you, Liz. You're *so* lucky."

"Thank you. Can't you just have the . . . bags or whatever they are removed?"

"Too late. Mike's bonded with them." She cast her eyes toward my kitchen. "Any food around here?"

"Chocolate pudding, some Jell-O—some chicken-with-rice soup."

She snooped around my kitchen area: butcher block counters and steel appliances—the sole luxurious addition the contractor made to the place. "Liz, you eat like you're on welfare. There's not one fresh anything in your whole kitchen." She opened and closed the fridge door. "And not even one magnet or photo on your fridge. Where's the Valentine's Day card Brianna made you? Are you trying to clinically depress your visitors?"

"I don't have visitors. You. Mother. William."

"Liz, *every*one has visitors."

"Not me."

She changed tack and removed the Pyrex bowl filled with Jell-O. "I'm going to eat your Jell-O. It's red. What flavour is it?"

"Red Jell-O is red Jell-O."

Her gold wrist jewellery clattered as she spooned down the goo I'd been saving for *Terms of Endearment*. She asked me, "Have you seen my bus stop yet?"

"Your *what?*"

"I have my own bus stop bench ad now, with a big black-and-white photo of me on it. Just one bench, but it's a start. It's a flattering shot, but we took it before I had my work done, so it doesn't seem like me any more."

"Where is it?"

"At Capilano Road and Keith, Canada's longest red light. A captive audience. I just know some little shit with a felt pen's going to go draw a Hitler moustache on it."

"Felt markers ought to be illegal."

"I agree. Kids today are monsters." She finished my Jell-O and somehow squeaked a drag from what remained of her cigarette. "Have to run."

"I think there's still one more spoonful left."

She was almost out the door. "You look like hell, darling. Three more days at least. Wouldn't you think?"

"Yes, Leslie. Thank you."

"See you tomorrow, darling."

I began to watch *Bambi.* I wasn't really sure why the video store clerk had recommended it as a sad movie—and it seemed pretty tame. There was a knock on my door, and because there was no intercom buzz I assumed it would be Wallace, the caretaker. It was young Donna from Landover Communication Systems, coltish and seemingly undernourished, standing in my hallway with a stack of folders and envelopes pressed to her chest. Everyone in the office likes Donna because she's always *up,* always on—but I'm on to her game. She's like me. She's a watcher.

"Donna?"

"Hello, Liz."

I realized how awful I must look. I touched my cheeks. "Swelling's pretty big."

She kept the papers clamped to her chest. "Liz, your eyes are all red."

"Sad movies."

"What?"

"Sad movies. Painkillers make them seem sadder than they really are."

"I love crying at sad movies."

"Oh. Would you like to come in?"

"Thank you."

"Liam said he was sending a courier."

"I thought it'd be better if I came instead."

Not only is Donna a watcher, she's also a minor tattle-tale, and she's no cretin. She scanned my apartment like it was so many bar-coded groceries. Doubtless the lunch-room was due for a guided playback the next day: *It's like a spinster's cellblock—almost nothing on the walls, furniture chosen by a colour-blind nun and, weirdest of all, no cats.*

Donna said, "Nice place."

"No it's not."

"Yes it is."

"It's adequate."

"I think it's nice."

"Are those the files Liam asked me to pick away at?"

"These?" She'd forgotten about them while she was doing her sweep. "Yes, they are. Nothing too complex, I hope. You must be kind of wooey from the drugs." She put the files on the dining table.

"Would you like some?"

She was shocked. "What—your drugs?"

"I was just kidding."

"Oh." She fished around for something to say, but my condo was almost entirely devoid of conversation fodder. On the TV screen she saw Thumper frozen on PAUSE. "You're watching *Bambi,* huh?"

I tried to be chatty. "You know, I'm thirty-six and I've never seen it before."

"It's so depressing. You know—Mrs. Bambi being shot and all."

This surprised me. "I didn't know that."

"You didn't know? Everybody knows that Bambi's mother gets shot. It's like Rudolph the Red-Nosed Reindeer—part of the culture."

I considered this. "You mean Rudolph the *Useful* Reindeer."

"Huh?"

"Let's be honest, if Rudolph hadn't been able to help the other reindeer, they'd have left him to the wolves—and laughed while the fangs punctured his hide."

"That's a grim way of looking at it."

I sighed and stared at the files Donna had brought me.

She changed the subject. She nodded at a Monet print of lilies at Giverny beside the kitchen. "Nice poster."

"My sister gave it to me."

"It suits you."

"It was left over when she redecorated her office."

Donna blew a fuse. "Liz, why do you have to be so negative? This is a great place. You ought to be happy with it. I live in a dump, and the rent's half my salary."

"Can I make you some coffee?"

"No, thanks. I have to head back to the office."

"You sure?"

"I have to go."

I saw her to the door and returned to the movie, and realized that knowing about Bambi's mother didn't spoil it. So I was happy.

At the end, I checked the year it was made: MCMXLII—1942. Even Bambi was long dead by now. He's soil, as are Thumper and Flower. Deer have up to an eighteen-year lifespan; rabbits, twelve; skunks, at most thirteen. And being soil doesn't sound like such a bad idea really, moist and granular like raspberry oatmeal muffins. Soil is alive—it has to be in order for it to nourish new life. So, in a way, it's not remotely deathlike. Burial is nice that way.

* * *

William, my older brother and possibly my best friend, waited until the evening to check up on me, right after *On the Beach*. In the truest sense of the word, I was sitting there speechless as the credits rolled and I contemplated an entire radioactive planet populated with decomposed bodies sitting in their offices, kitchens, in cars and on front lawns. When he came in, I don't even think I said hello—I merely sniffled, but the *verklempt* mood fled the moment I saw my two essentially evil nephews, Hunter and Chase, run in after him.

"Lizzie, Jesus, your eyes look like two piss holes in the snow. I can't stay long. I have to fly to London on a red-eye."

"Hello, William."

The twins groaned in harmony, "We're hu*nnnnnnn*gry," followed by Chase saying to his father, making no attempt to masquerade his feelings, "Aunt Lizzie's place blows. You said we could go to the arcade."

I said, "Hello, Hunter. Hello, Chase," who, as usual, ignored me.

William addressed his sons. "Well, if I'd told you we were going to Lizzie's, then I'd never have gotten you into the car."

"You lied!"

"I did not, and if—and only *if*—you behave, I might still take you to your arcade, so shut the crap up and leave us alone." William then glanced at me: "I'm turning into Father," he said.

"Turning? You're already there."

The twins had invaded the kitchen and spotted the remains. "Any more Jell-O left?"

"No."

"I hate coming here."

"Thank you, Chase. Have some pudding."

"We can't eat dairy."

I looked at William. "Since when?"

"It's from Nancy's side of the family," he said.

"Have some crackers, boys. They're in the second drawer from the top."

They looked, saw it was only saltines and slammed the drawer shut. "Hunter, let's watch TV." Chase was always the leader.

Within moments, they'd colonized my couch and barnacled themselves onto a pro wrestling event. The noise was cheap and booming, but at least it shut them up.

"You didn't have to come visit, William. I'm fine. It's just wisdom teeth."

"Mother said you looked pretty bad. And pretty depressed, too."

"She did?"

"It smells like an ashtray in here."

"I smoke sometimes. And Leslie came for a visit."

"That would explain it. Let's open those godawful curtains. Where'd you find them—a Greek bingo hall?"

The curtains came with the place. They were mustard yellow, with orange-and-gold brocade, and I suspect the contractor's wife chose them.

"William, stop. I know how dreary it is, okay?" Was my place really *that* depressing? On the carpet I saw two small, faint ovals from where I over-cleaned bits of the carpet—a slice of pizza that landed the wrong way, and a Sharpie pen I dropped while wrapping Christmas presents.

"Nancy couldn't make it. She sends her wishes," my brother said.

"Send her mine as well." This was a joke, as William's wife, Nancy, and I don't tolerate each other. I told her once at Thanksgiving that she wore too much perfume. Her riposte was that my hair looked like a toupée, and our relationship never recovered. This kind of rift only ever widens.

A squawk came from the couch. Chase had pushed a button on the remote that somehow obliterated the TV's ability to receive a cable signal, and white noise blared at full volume, setting my remaining teeth on edge. The boys argued over whose fault it was, and then screamed about how to fix it, finally deigning to ask me. I pretended not to know, in hopes it might speed their departure. William manually turned off the TV, and swatted each of the boys on the back of the head. "We're in someone else's house, you little jerks." The boys began to sniffle, but then William said, "Nice try, you little crybabies. Tears may work on your mother, but don't try that on me, okay?" He turned to me. "Jesus, Lizzie, do you have any Scotch or something?"

"Baileys. From Christmas."

"Why not?"

Chase asked, "What's Baileys?"

"Something you're not getting," his father replied.

The boys went quiet, too quiet. The room's air felt warm and bloated, just waiting for a lightning bolt—which I then delivered. I said, "Did your father ever tell you that I once found a dead body?"

Their eyes bulged. "What?" They looked to William for confirmation.

"Yes, she did."

"Where? When?"

"Lizzie, it was in, what, grade six?"

"Five. I was the same age as you two are now."

"How?"

William said, "If you two would just shut up, maybe we'll find out."

I handed my brother his Baileys. "I was walking on the railway tracks."

"Where?"

"Out by Horseshoe Bay."

Hunter asked, "By yourself?"

Chase looked at me and said, "Aunt Lizzie, do you have *friends?*"

I said, "Yes, *thank you,* Chase. In any event, it was summer, and I was picking blackberries—by myself. I rounded a corner and I saw a shirt in the fireweed on an embankment. People huck all sorts of things from trains—mostly juice boxes and pop cans—so I didn't pay it too much attention. But as I walked closer, I saw some more colour there—a shirt and then shoes. And then I realized it was a man."

* * *

That much was true. It was indeed a man, but I only gave the boys my PG-13 version of the event. They were the same age I had been when it happened, but somehow Chase and Hunter seemed younger than their years. Look at me—here I am being biased against them in the same way people were against me throughout the dead body episode.

Here's what happened: It was August and I'd been quite happy to be by myself for the entire afternoon, taking several buses out to Horseshoe Bay, having a quick cheeseburger at a concession stand near the ferry terminal, and then hiking up steep hills and piles of blasted rock to the PGE rail line. I was wearing a blue-and-white gingham dress, which I hated, but it kept me cool, and a day's walk on the rails would kill it with oils and chemicals and dirt, so I could live with it for one more day. You might ask, what was a twelve-year-old girl doing alone in a semi-remote place near a big city? Simple answer: it was the seventies. Past a certain age, children just did their thing, with little concern shown by their parents for what, where, when or with whom. Chase and Hunter probably have chips embedded in their tailbones linked up to a Microsoft death-satellite that informs William and Nancy where they are at all times. But back then?

"Mom, is it okay if I hitchhike to the biker bar?"

"Sure, dear."

It was a baking July day, all scents were amplified, and I smelled something quite awful. Actually, I immediately guessed that the odour was that of a partially decomposed body. Knowledge of this smell must be innate. As I approached it, I was almost happy; I liked to think a short lifetime of detective novels, TV shows and secret visions had prepared me for this moment. A crime to solve. Clues to locate.

I'd never seen a dead body before. Kids at school had seen car crashes, which made me jealous, but this? This was *murder,* and a grisly one at that. The man's body had been severed at the waist, the two halves positioned at a right angle. The corpse's lower half was wearing a floral print skirt and knee-high boots, and the top half was wearing a plaid lumberjack shirt. The face was untouched, a quite handsome man's face, grey at this point, in spite of thick makeup: flaking foundation, mascara and one false eyelash, still attached. Flies buzzed all around. I wondered who this man had been, and why he'd been wearing a skirt.

The skirt. Here's something shameful I've never told anybody before: I took a piece of alder branch, stripped it of leaves and then went over to the lower half of the body. I needed to lift up the skirt and see whether the—well, whether the bottom half went with the top—and it did—with no underwear, either.

Who could have done this to him? I looked around, and nary a weed or daisy stem nearby had been bent or bloodied. There was no evidence that the cutting and splattering had occurred on location. Even to a twelve-year-old, it was pretty obvious the body had been dumped. I stood there in the heat, suddenly thirsty. I remember that it was the corpse's makeup that confused me more than the body, or even the skirt.

I am not a callous person, and have never been. I imagine most people might have vomited or looked away, but I simply didn't. That's how coroners must feel. I can only imagine that one is, or is not, born with squeamishness. Surgery scenes on TV? I'm in. To be blunt, finding the body seemed to affect me about as much as an uncooked roast.

And also—and this is something I didn't pinpoint until years later—being that close to something so totally dead made me feel . . . infinite—immortal.

I was standing there immobile for maybe five minutes before I heard a train off in the distance, coming from the north, from Squamish. It was the Royal Hudson, an old-fashioned steam train refurbished and converted into a tourist attraction, chugging down the Howe Sound fjord. I stood beside the body amid the fireweed, chamomile and dandelions to await the train's approach. I kept looking between the body and the bend in the track around which the train would come, as the steaming and chugging came closer and closer.

Finally, the Royal Hudson huffed around the bend. I stood in the middle of the tracks, the scent of creosote from the trestles burning my nostrils, and waved my arms. The conductor later said he almost popped a blood vessel seeing me there. He clamped on the brakes, and the squealing was unlike any noise I'd heard until then. It was so shrill it collapsed time and space. I think that was the moment I stopped being a child. Not the corpse, but the noise.

The engine stopped a few cars past the body and me. The conductor, whose name was Ben, and his partner jumped down, cursing me for pulling such a prank. I simply pointed at the severed body.

"What the—? Barry. Come over here." Ben looked at me. "Kid, get away from this thing."

"No."

"Look, kiddo, I said—"

I just stared at him.

Barry came over, took a look and promptly vomited. Ben came closer, and he dealt with the corpse simply by not looking at it. Meanwhile, I couldn't look at it enough. He said, "Jesus, kid—are you some sort of freak?"

"I found him. He's mine."

Barry radioed the authorities from the engine. Of course, the tourists were gawking from the train's windows, snapping away. I suppose these days photos would be posted on the Internet within hours, but back then there was only the local papers, none of which were allowed to publish either news or photos of the body until the next of kin had been found and notified. And so, while the passengers tried to hop out of the cars to check out the action, Barry was able to feel useful screaming at them to get back in. By the time the authorities arrived, he had the cheese-grater voice of an aged starlet.

The police asked me questions. Had I moved anything? Had I seen anyone? I kept my peeled alder switch a secret. But other than having found the body, my role was limited. I just watched it all. The one question they didn't ask was, *Why would my parents allow me to pick blackberries so far away from home all by myself?* Again, it was the 1970s.

The police complimented me on my coolness, and once the scene calmed down a bit, Ben offered me a ride in the engine back to the PGE station in North Vancouver. The police wanted to drive me home, but I pleaded my case and was able to ride the train. I have yet to equal the sense of mastery over my destiny I had during that experience. Me at the helm of this million-pound chunk of fate, pounding along an iron track—God help whoever stood in my way. It was supreme. I was alive! I was not a corpse!

Nobody was home to witness my enigmatic arrival in a strange man's car. It wasn't until I had to jump up to reach for the house key in its hiding spot on the top brick that I realized I'd clutched my Tupperware container of blackberries perfectly level for over four hours, with not a single berry spilled.

When I told my story at the dinner table, everybody just rolled their eyes and assumed I was being morbid. Mother said, "You need to be around people your own age more."

"I don't like people my own age."

"Of course you do. You simply don't know it yet."

"All the girls my own age do is shoplift and smoke."

Dad said, "No more dead body stories, dear."

"It's not made up."

Leslie said, "Tanya wants to be a stewardess after school ends."

"The body is *real.*" I went to the phone and dialed the police station. How many fifth-grade students know the phone number of the local police station by heart? I asked for Officer Nairne to confirm my tale.

Father took the phone. "Whoever this is, I'm sorry, but Liz— What? Oh. Really? Well I'll be darned." I had newly found respect.

Father hung up the phone and sat back down. "It seems our Liz is on the money."

William and Leslie wanted gory details. "How far gone was he, Lizzie?"

"Blue cheese gone?"

"William!" Mother was being genteel. "Not at the dinner table."

"It actually looked like the roast pork we're eating here."

Mother said, "Liz, stop right now!"

Father added, "And you weren't going to eat those blackberries, were you? I saw them in the fridge. The railways spray the worst sorts of herbicides along the right-of-ways. You'll get cancer from them."

There was a charged silence. "Come on, everybody, I found a body today. Why can't we just talk about it?"

William asked, "Was he bloated?"

"No. He'd only been there overnight. But he was wearing a skirt."

Mother said, "Liz! We can discuss this afterwards, but not, I repeat *not,* at the dinner table."

Father said, "I think you're overreac—"

"Leslie, how was swim class?"

So there was my big moment, gone. But as of that night I began to believe I had second sight that allowed me to see corpses wherever they lay buried. I saw bodies everywhere: hidden in blackberry thickets, beneath lawns, off the sides of trails in parks—the world was one big corpse factory. Visiting the cemetery in Vancouver for my grandmother's funeral a year later was almost like a drug. I could not only see the thousands of dead, but I began to be able to see who was fresh and who wasn't. The fresh bodies still had a glow about them while the older ones, well, their owners had gone wherever it was they were headed. For me, looking at a cemetery was like looking at a giant stack of empties waiting to be handed in for a refund.

Bodies. Oh, *groan.* I've always just wanted to leave this body of mine. What a treat that would be! To be a beam of light, a little comet, jiggling itself loose from these wretched bones. My inner beauty could shine and soar! But no, my body is my test in life.

* * *

William hustled the boys out after I finished the tale of the body. For once in their lives their Aunt Liz had, for a moment or two, fascinated them. I suspect that for a time Hunter and Chase thought I was a sorceress, too, albeit a boring sorceress with no food in her fridge.

My relief that they'd gone was akin to unzipping my pants after a huge meal: it was one of those few moments that being by myself didn't mean I had to feel lonely. When I think about it, I've never actually told another person I'm lonely. Whom would I tell—Donna? Everyone in the coffee room? Leslie and William, who feel duty bound to keep checking in on their spinster sister? I maintain a good front. I imagine the people in my life driving in their cars discussing me . . .

Is Liz lonely?

I don't think so.

I think she's like one of nature's castoffs.

She genuinely enjoys not being around people.

She's very brave in her own way.

Books always tell me to find "solitude," but I've Googled their authors, and they all have spouses and kids and grandkids, as well as fraternity and sorority memberships. The universally patronizing message of the authors is, "Okay, I got lucky and found someone to be with, but if I'd hung in there just a *wee* bit longer, I'd have achieved the blissful solitude you find me writing about in this book." I can just imagine the faces of these writers, sitting at their desks as they write their sage platitudes, their faces stoic and wise: "Why be lonely when you can enjoy solitude?"

Gee, in a lifetime of singleness I've never once toyed with the notion of locating solitude for myself.

I've checked out all the books on the subject, books ranging from the trailer park to the ivory tower: *Finding Your Achey-Breaky Soulmate* to *Deconstructing the Inner Dialogue—Methodologies of Navigating the Postmodern Self.* The writers of these books that tout loneliness cures universally trot out a dusty list of authors through history who have dared to discuss loneliness as a topic, but they could never just say *loneliness.* It has to be a tree or butterfly or pond—dead nineteenth-century gay guys who wrote about trees and lakes and who probably had huge secret worlds that they never wrote about. Or . . .

It occurs to me that I sound like a bitter old bag.

But when your central nervous system is constantly firing away like a diesel generator, relentlessly overpowering subtle or fine emotions, how are you supposed to derive solace from stories of oneness with nature written by those old-fashioned writers, about hiking and breezes in the trees? If they were alive today, they'd all be in leather bars.

* * *

A day passed. I was still drugged, but it wasn't fun or *verklempt*ish any more. By Friday morning my face had shrunk back to its old shape. I'd run out of videos, and I was tempted to phone Liam and ask to come back to work for the day. But then, around seven in the morning, the phone rang. It was the RCMP, asking if I could come to Lions Gate Hospital.

"Excuse me?"

"There's been an incident, Ms. Dunn."

"An incident? What? Who?"

"Do you know a Jeremy Buck, Ms. Dunn?"

"Jeremy Buck?" It's not like my memory bank of contacts is very big, so I was quick to say no. "What does this have to do with me?"

"If you could just come to the hospital, Ms. Dunn. We had a young man brought in here last night, an overdose case with some bruising and a few cuts."

"What?"

"He had no ID on him, but he had a MedicAlert bracelet around his wrist saying that, should anything happen to him, you were the person to be notified. It had your phone number on it. Which is how we came to contact you."

In one searing moment it dawned on me who Jeremy was. This was the phone call I'd never allowed myself to imagine.

"Ms. Dunn?"

"Sorry . . ."

"Ms. Dunn, can you—"

"I'll be there in thirty minutes."

The officer told me the hospital room and wing numbers.

I'd always wondered if this day would ever come. It felt like the fulfillment of a prophecy. My mind was blank while I went through the motions—dressing, going to the car, driving along Marine, Fifteenth, St. George's, then entering the parking lot, walking in through the automated hospital doors—the elevator, the smell of disinfectant, the harried staff.

When I asked the reception desk nurse about which hospital wing was Jeremy's, she signalled an RCMP constable toward us. He told me his name was Ray Chung, a nice man who shook my hand and asked me to follow him. And so I did, down a yellow-lit hall and around a corner, mostly staring at his feet marching ahead of me on the polished aggregate flooring. We entered a darkened room, passing through a veil of thin and overly washed blue curtain.

A doctor stood in front of some venetian louvre blinds. She was clearly impatient, and her head was haloed by the dozens of hair wisps that had escaped hours ago from her bun. "I'm Valerie, Dr. Tyson. I'm the duty doctor. This guy here related to you?"

Constable Chung nodded toward the man on the bed—a handsome guy, early twenties, large, fair skin, with dark, slightly curly hair and just enough of my family's head shape to quash any doubts about who he was. *This was him. This is who he turned out to be.*

I walked over and touched his hand. This woke him up, and he started: "It's *you.*"

"Yes, it's me."

He sat up and looked around the room. "Wait—something kind of weird happened here."

"What?"

"I think I was dead."

What was he talking about? "As far as I could tell, you were only asleep."

"No. I was dead. I know I was."

I looked at Dr. Tyson, who said, "Technically, Jeremy, you *were* dead, for maybe a minute or so when you first came in this morning." She looked at me. "Around five."

I was surprised. "He was *dead?*"

"We used the paddles on him." She made a hand gesture like a defibrillator.

I looked back at Jeremy, who seemed disturbed. "I didn't see the light—you know—that *light* you're supposed to see when you die. I just saw a blob of darkness, and I was being pulled into it."

None of us in the room knew what to say to this, so Dr. Tyson used medical science to stabilize the mood, to make it clinical. "We found traces of cocaine and Rohypnol in your system. That might account for anything unusual you may have seen."

Jeremy was mad now. "*May* have seen? I was being pulled down, down into the earth. I wasn't going up into any light. There was no light for *me*."

I took hold of his hand, which was freezing cold. The bracelet looked more like a dog tag than jewellery. "Jeremy, look at me," I said, saying his name out loud for the first time. "How long have you been wearing this bracelet on your wrist?"

"Four years."

"Four *years?*"

"And a bit."

"And you didn't call me?"

"No, but don't take it that way. I didn't call because you've always been my hope—the ace up my sleeve."

"But you don't *know* me. How can you say that?"

"I know enough about you."

"How?" I couldn't imagine what this must've sounded like to Dr. Tyson and Constable Chung.

Jeremy said, "I did legwork."

"How do you mean?"

"I, well, I sort of followed you around."

"You *what?*"

"Relax—it's not scary like it sounds."

"Yes, it is."

"No. You're looking at it the wrong way."

"What's the right way?"

"The right way is this: I've been with so many screwed-up foster families in my life that before I went to meet my real family, I wanted to make sure you weren't a psychopath like the rest of them."

This struck me as a pretty good reason. It also shut me up.

"I know where you work and where the rest of the family is. All that stuff. The basics."

I said nothing; he had every right to be wary. Constable Chung coughed. Dr. Tyson hadn't left; overworked or not, this was truly something.

Jeremy said, "Liz—*Mom*. You like to think of yourself as a rock—that you're tough and nobody can hurt you, but you're wrong there." He stopped. I had the strange notion that something in his head had just melted and made a stain of some kind. "I think I'm fading here," he said, and closed his eyes.

Dr. Tyson checked his pulse, looked at me and the cop, and told us he should probably sleep awhile.

"Can I stay here?" I asked.

"Sure."

Jeremy was instantly asleep, and what could I do but sit there silently, now holding the chilly hand of my own son? On a chair I saw a pile of silly-looking mesh stockings and black lingerie. Constable Chung saw me looking and said, "Uh, we found him in those, and he was all made up. The nurse cleaned him up."

I recalled the body I saw when I was twelve, the blackberries; the body clothed in something abnormal; the creosote stink of railway trestles.

Taking a look at my face, the doctor volunteered, "I think it was actually a costume for *The Rocky Horror Picture Show*. They do midnight screenings at the Ridge Theatre. I used to go to them back when they were happening the first time around."

"Is he going to be okay?" I asked her.

"This time, yes. Next time—maybe. The time after that? Who knows?"

Unarguable logic. Jeremy's hand was warming up. I looked at Chung and he shrugged. "You've never met your own son?"

"No."

"You're kidding."

"No. I mean, I knew he—Jeremy—was out there, but not . . ." But not *what? But not this beautiful man here in front of me.*

"How old is he?"

"Twenty."

"Twenty?"

The hiss of oxygen in the tube beneath my son's nose—it took me back to Rome. It carried me back two decades to the night where fat, plain, Canadian *me* stood in the rain on a rooftop near the Colosseum. I was sixteen, and it was the era of acid rain—a subject that seems long forgotten now. The skies of Europe showered battery acid back then. I remembered looking out over the Colosseum and its neighbourhood, under a pigeon-feather grey sky, quite late on a weeknight, all traffic noises gone. The acid rain was falling on the city's marble and travertine monuments, and I imagined I could hear them hiss and crackle under the acid, dissolving more in one year than they had in a thousand, history melting away before my eyes. And this was the oxygen ventilator's noise.

I moved in closer to Jeremy and kissed him on the cheek.

* * *

That I had wanted to travel anywhere, let alone Rome, had sent a shock through the family dinner table. To most ears a Latin class excursion sounds like the pinnacle of dullness. Not quite so. The class actually had a somewhat dark mix of students, a blend of linguistic geeks, rebellious sons of literary parents, and cool-headed girls with their efficient eyes focused on being MDs one day. It was the only fun class I ever had.

Leslie, recently graduated and in and out of home at whim, was our family's traveller—a ten-day tour of southern England in ninth grade and three weeks in Nova Scotia as a B & B chambermaid the summer after she graduated, both trips drenched in sex and scandal.

"Rome?" said Father. "That's yesterday's world. Go to Tomorrow. Go to Houston—San Diego—Atlanta." Father was only interested in making new things. To him, a fifteenth-century church would be nothing more than a shell on a beach.

"You're too young to go anywhere," said Mother.

William, a year older than Leslie, said, "Sixteen is fine. And what—like she's going to hop off the plane and be instantly molested? Come *on.*"

"But those Italians . . ." My mother wasn't so sure that my plump frumpiness rendered me asexual.

"They're no different than the English, Mother. Men are men. Face it." That Leslie, aged eighteen, could say something this daring-yet-clichéd at the dinner table, and have it accepted as gospel, testified to her unshakeable faith in the power of her own allure, and to my lack thereof.

"I suppose you're right," Mother caved in. "What about money?"

"I'll pay," I said. "I've never spent any of my babysitting or paper route money."

"What?" My brother was clearly astonished. "That's so depressing. *None* of it? Not even a blouse? A Chap Stick?"

"Nothing."

Leslie asked, "What'll you wear?"

Father said, "Whoa, Nellie! Who said Lizzie was even going?"

"Oh, *hush,* Neil," Mother replied. "It'll broaden her horizons." Again she spoke as if I wasn't there: "The poor thing doesn't even have any posters up in her room."

"Fair enough."

That I was paying for the trip myself was all my pragmatic, rules-oriented father really needed to know.

My parents . . . I suppose one could call them generic. In the absence of any overarching quirks or pathologies, they had ended up defaulting on the side of cheapness, dirt management and chore scheduling—which is to say, they ended up like most parents. Father had his garage, off the floor of which you could, if you wished, eat one of my mother's economically prepared meals at precisely six o'clock every night, cardigan sweaters optional but preferred.

My father was killed in 1985, when I was twenty-five. He fell asleep at the wheel driving into Honolulu on the 78, ramming headfirst into an Isuzu truck with three local kids in the cab. Mother was unhurt, and remembers none of it. Funny—he seems so far away to me now. He never spoke much, and as a result I have few memories. Below a certain point, if you keep too quiet, people no longer see you as thoughtful or deep; they simply forget you. In any event, at the airport he handed me five hundred dollars in lire, which for him was the equivalent of a normal person renting a biplane to spell out a goodbye in the sky. He was essentially a kind man.

Back at the dinner table that night, Leslie said, "I think I have some jumbo oversize sweaters that just might fit you."

"*Thank* you, Leslie."

"You'll have hickeys all over your bum from being pinched." William was attempting to be gallant in his way, flattering my young mind that, no matter what, I could still be wanted, however slim the odds.

Mother said, "Stop that, William. The Latin class sponsors this trip, not your friends with their hot rods. I might add, last week I was driving a bit too slowly on Cross Creek and your friend Allan Blake gave me the finger. He didn't know it was me, but I knew it was him, and I never want to see him here again, you hear?"

William was still focused on my trip. "I bet you fall for some guy who works at a Fiat factory."

"Marcello," added Leslie, "a fiery idealist. Chianti bottles. A sweaty undershirt—picnics beside the *autostrada*—"

"He slaps you around a bit. He gets jealous easily—"

"But you'd kill for him—"

"Stop!" My mother was appalled at how sexualized her two eldest children were. The only comfort she seemed to find was my incontestable virginity. "Lizzie is going to go to Rome, and she is going to learn about the great works of art there, and . . . eat *Roman* food, and . . ." Words temporarily failed her. " . . . become a serious and scholarly young woman."

Even my own spirits were dampened by such a clinical vision of Rome. Truth was, I wanted to see naked statues of people because I was too embarrassed to pick up certain magazines in certain stores, the ones in the part of town it took me three bus transfers to reach. I always wimped out and stayed up front reading the knitting catalogues. Why they even bothered stocking catalogues up front is beyond me. The real clientele of those places always lurked at the store's rear, exclusively men, clad in raincoats, toupées and shame.

To me, the thought of Rome—a city adorned with genitalia rather than vinyl siding and stucco—seemed improbable. I had to see this place. In the weeks leading up to the trip's charter airline departure, I kept waiting for a TV studio's buzzer to sound, for an audience to shriek at me, telling me that it was all a big prank.

* * *

Jeremy and I were alone in the hospital room well into the night, save for the sinister hiss of his oxygen, a speaker system squawking in another wing or the rare motorcycle gunning its engine on the road below. Jeremy's eyes stayed shut. I wondered what I was going to say when he opened them—but it turned out I didn't have to worry about that. Around three a.m., he opened them and said, "My name isn't written in the Book of Life."

I had no idea what he was talking about, but answered, "Don't be stupid. Of course it is."

"No—you don't understand—when they paddled me back here, I was already falling on my way to hell. I was yanked, like I was bungeed, back into this building." He squeezed my wrist, as if taking my pulse. "It sucked the air out of me."

"Jeremy, you're not going to hell." My son had no apparent aptitude for small talk, but that was fine, for nor do I. I said, "All that happened was that last night you did some very stupid party drugs, and now you're paying the price. That stuff fries the wiring in your head like booster cables."

"Let's change the subject."

"Done."

We sat there feeling foolish.

Jeremy asked, "So, have you been preparing a speech to give me inside your head for the past twenty years?"

"Of course. You, too?"

"Yup."

There was more silence, happier this time.

I said, "Neither of us is going to give the speech, right?"

"It'd be kind of corny."

"It would."

"I feel much better already."

I asked, "How did you find me? I tried locating you for years with no luck. The government was really prickish about it."

"Well, it's amazing what you can find in this world if you're willing to sleep with people." He said this as if he were giving me a household hint.

"I suppose so."

"I'd be a good spy."

"I didn't notice you spying on me for four years, so yes. When was the last time you ate?"

"As in food?"

"No, as in tractors. Of *course* I mean food."

"I had a ninety-three-cent piece of pizza yesterday. At noon." The unusual pizza price was a local merchandising twist; with tax, a slice came to one dollar.

"Those ninety-three-cent slices are about as good for you as a roasted bandage."

"I swiped a block of mozzarella from the supermarket on Davie."

"What on earth does that have to do with anything?"

"Everything. So long as a block of cheese is still vacuum-sealed, the pizzerias accept them as currency. They give you a free slice, and maybe five bucks."

"You'd risk a police record for five bucks and a microwaved Band-Aid?"

"It's okay. The supermarket gives you two options if they catch you—one: they call the cops, and two: they take a

Polaroid of you holding up whatever it was you shoplifted. It's almost always cheese. And then they tell you never to come back into the store. They have this whole back wall covered with faded photos of street scum holding cheeses. It's not as if I'm risking a police record. Merely a ritual humiliation."

This was genuinely interesting to me. I said so.

"I bet you something."

"What? What do you bet me?"

"I bet you think I'm street trash."

I sighed. "Well, Jeremy, let me check my data so far: drugs; overdose; mesh stockings; cheese theft . . ."

"I *used* to be street trash."

"Okay. Sure."

"But I stopped being trash a few years ago."

"I'm glad to hear that." I considered this. "Can you do that? I mean, just stop that whole way of life?"

"Yes. Or I thought I could. Until last night. My friend Jane got me all dragged up for the *Rocky Horror* show."

"So your doctor told me."

"*Tyson?* Man, from what I just saw, she needs a morphine drip and a lost weekend with a tennis pro. She's one of those doctors who overdoes it. I can tell with one blink."

"I think you may be right."

"What's with the puffy face?"

"I had my wisdom teeth taken out four days ago."

"Pain?"

"No. They gave me lots of drugs."

"Any leftovers?"

"No!" I pretend-swatted him.

"Never hurts to try."

I asked him how he felt. He went quiet. I said, "*Hello?*"

He pulled into himself, just like that, his shine *gone*.

"Jeremy? Here you are, sick and all, and we're discussing . . . stolen cheese. That's stupid. Sorry."

His fingers tightened onto mine. As with my bowl of blackberries on the railway, I'd not even noticed we'd been holding hands the whole time.

I asked, "Jeremy—should I find a nurse?"

He shook his head, no, with an intensity that surprised me.

"What's going on? Tell me."

"It's bad stuff. Not good stuff at all."

"What isn't good stuff—the darkness you talked about?"

"No. In my life. Where I've lived."

"Your family—families?"

"That would be part of it. I sometimes get hijacked by pictures."

"Pictures of what?"

"Omens. Things we see when we're near the end times."

Oh God, just when we get onto our feet and walking, some weird new bit of his personality derails things.

"—burning whales heaving themselves onto beaches, daisies that shatter, bales of money that wash up on shore; trees that go limp and deflate . . ."

I wondered if he was still high, but he anticipated me. "I'm not high. That stuff wore off hours ago."

"I'm not a religious person, Jeremy."

"I can run—*we* can run—but we can't hide."

"From . . . ?"

"The mandate of heaven."

Nothing in my life had prepared me for this situation, so I simply kept quiet.

He said, "I'm a leper. I need a leper messiah." He looked at me. "That's David Bowie."

"Ziggy Stardust. Yes, I remember."

He looked out the blinded windows. "This fallen world is going to end, but at least I saw it before the fall."

"I suppose."

"It can be so beautiful, you know—earth, I mean."

"Look, Jeremy—I, uh—I'm not like you. I have a hard time understanding beauty." I thought maybe Jeremy was lonely like me. Perhaps loneliness was genetic. Maybe, but he tried to make his loneliness shimmer, while my own loneliness flickered like a failing fluorescent tube.

He said, "I'm just pulling your leg with all this stuff, you know."

"Why would you do that?"

"Keeps things interesting." He looked back out the window. "I have to sleep now."

"Then go to sleep."

"Will you be sitting here when I wake up?"

I thought about this. "Yes," I said.

"Nighty-night."

* * *

In the weeks following my discovery of the dead guy I stewed away, mad that the local police force wasn't at all interested in having me help them locate clues and help them solve the crime. I figured that, having discovered him, I was naturally entitled to do so. I felt that the police were unforthcoming with details of a crime which to my mind screamed tabloid: transvestite lumberjack, found severed in two, on the PGE tracks just north of Horseshoe Bay. I suspect the West Van police had call screening long before the general public; they always seemed to know it was me phoning, and the receptionist was only ever condescending. I started taking buses down to the WVPD offices, where I was condescended to in person. So I began visiting other cop shops in other jurisdictions across town, asking to speak with someone, anyone, who'd listen. The plan was successful, but unintentionally so. The police must have found it funny, a chubby little girl showing up and demanding to help solve a crime across town. What a chance to josh colleagues I must have been.

When I finally got a response from the local police, it made me feel vindicated. It didn't last long. Two officers showed up at our door. They told me what they could of the crime—not much—and then asked my parents to try and rope me in. Did my parents champion me? No. Their part of the dialogue was more along the lines of

We should have sent her to camp.

When does school start?

Too much time, and not enough to do.

We're sorry, officers, we'll try to make sure she doesn't bother you again.

Of course, as I was pursuing news of my corpse, my siblings were getting stoned, sexually dabbling, doing donuts in the mall parking lot after closing time, breaking into subdivision homes for thrills, decanting Father's Smirnoff and making up the difference with tap water, shooting convertibles with BB guns, shoplifting autumn clothing. In their way they were inspiring.

Shortly after my final trip to hound the police, I was walking around our neighbourhood scouting red huckleberries when I stopped in front of the Adamses' house, about ten up from ours. I knew the Adams kids were away in Alberta, and that Mr. and Mrs. Adams both worked. Before I knew it, I was walking up the driveway and knocking on the front door. I figured that if someone answered, I'd say I was looking for the kids. But nobody answered. I went around to the garage and knocked on the kitchen door there, but again no answer. I tried the knob with my hand. The door was open—and so in I went.

Oh, the sensation of being all alone in a place I wasn't supposed to be! It was fragrant: somebody *else's* house. It reminded me of coming home from vacation and walking in the door of my own house, and smelling it as if I was a stranger entering for the first time. I felt like a police officer, investigating clues. I felt like a ghost who had come back, not to haunt, but merely to remember the world as it once was.

From that first venture into the Adamses' house, my summers unfolded as long dull stretches punctuated by the occasional B and E. I'd walk up and down the mountain, find a house with no cars in the carport, walk up to the front door and ring the doorbell. If nobody answered, I'd try the door, and two times out of three it was unlocked. I'd open the door and shout, *Kelly? Kelly, are you in?* My logic was that, if someone answered, I could pretend I'd rung the wrong doorbell. Even if I ran away, the worst that could happen would be . . . nothing. I didn't look like a criminal and, technicalities aside, I wasn't one. I just wanted to be in a place where I wasn't supposed to be, I wanted quiet and I wanted something to do. Snooping in drawers was always the most fun, with bedrooms being the biggest trove. To snoop inside a person's bedside drawer is to take a carnival barker's tour through their deepest self. The things people stash there!—knives, brass knuckles, pills, condoms, old love letters, birth control pills, gold coins, pornography, passports, wills, and, in one case, a Luger.

Obviously, I was perpetually on the listen for a car driving in or a door latch opening, and there was only ever one narrow escape—somebody dropping a set of keys on a kitchen table down a hallway. I hopped through a back window and into a salmonberry shrub—a shame, since I'd really been enjoying leafing through a family photo album, trying to figure out who was related to whom, and who were going to be the family's winners and losers, and, obviously, figuring out who was cute and who wasn't. But during all those B and Es, I *never* looked at the porn—yes, even sitting there by myself, opening the pages was too hard. *This,* from a girl who looked up the skirt of a drag queen's corpse. But *that* was death; *this* was sex. As I said, in order to look at nude bodies I still had to make several bus transfers across town, and even there I always choked and ended up in the front reading *Newsweek* and knitting catalogues.

* * *

Everybody but me on the charter flight to Italy seemed to be in love, or to be searching for it as if it were a new restaurant they'd heard about. Elliot, the class thug, was in love with Colleen, the future ear-nose-throat doctor, who was in love with Alain, the future Volvo dealer, who loved

Christy Parks, the future plant nursery saleswoman, and so on. Fifteen years later, I learned that Christy's someone else was our Latin teacher, Mr. Burden. I bumped into them as they were buying croissants on Granville Island on an overcast Saturday afternoon amid cranky seagulls, bored tourists, bagels and mimes. Mr. Burden had kept his wavy hair in a way that made me think he was vain about it, but he was now chubby to the point where he probably had to go to a men's big-and-tall store. Christy was her old self, with maybe seven grey hairs and skin that spoke of too much time in the sun. We went for coffee to reminisce about the school trip to Italy. Christy had never been unkind to me, but nor had she ever been friendly. Her current kindness was unexpected.

Reminiscing about our flight there, she said, "Oh! It was so brutal. Everyone smoking, the airplane seats were the size of letter paper, and that astronaut food they served us—my gut was a disaster the whole time in Rome."

"So was mine."

"But I snagged my teacher in the end."

Mr. Burden was hasty to inject, "We met at a line dancing class. Nothing inappropriate happened on that trip."

I said, "Remember that horrible little gas station?" Our hostel's toilets had been plugged with what was essentially papier mâché. As the country's plumbers were on strike that month, we had to find other options.

"How could I forget? And the guys who worked there—never seen any better, before or since."

Mr. Burden looked at Christy. "You never told me any of this." He sipped his Americano. "I almost gave myself cancer from stress on that trip. It was the last school trip I did.

I had to make sure none of you brats were kidnapped or killed, though it might have taught you a lesson."

There followed an awkward pause, during which Christy looked at my ringless fingers. "Have you been married, Liz?"

"Me? No. Not yet. Never fell in love."

"Huh."

Take it from me—the moment most people in relationships find out you're single, their eyes start to wander. I thought I'd try to grab their attention. "You know, my own theory on love comes from a TV game show." They both gave me their Liz-is-a-freak stare. "It's not as if I spend my life watching game shows, but when I do, I remember everything," I said.

"Really, now?"

"Oh yes. One show I caught asked the contestants how many times the average person thinks people are able to fall in love during their lifetime. The answer was six."

Christy said, "Six?"

Mr. Burden—Dan—said, "That sounds a bit . . . excessive. How did they measure that?"

"I have no idea, but no wonder people have affairs. They have all of these unused love credits inside them, and they want to use them up before they die." I could tell from the looks that Christy and Dan swapped that I'd pushed a button, but I've never found out which one. They abruptly stood, coffees left unfinished.

Christy said, "It was fun seeing you again, Liz."

Mr. Burden was clearly annoyed at Christy—over what, I'll never know—but he said a gruff goodbye and they were off into the packs of scavenging birds, dithering people and buskers singing Neil Young songs out of key.

I thought about how different Mr. Burden had been back in school. He was the Latin teacher who had to teach PE—he was never without thick white terry cloth socks and a nickel-plated whistle dangling across his grey kangaroo jacket. I was barely a blip on his radar; he only began remembering my name about halfway through my second year with him. When I raised my hand, it seemed to annoy him just because it was me and not somebody else.

Don't start thinking, *Oh, just another case of low self-esteem.* I've never disliked myself. In my teens, I was merely clueless. Nobody had ever sat me down and told me about the currency of looks and bodies and—in later life—about money and power. William and Leslie, masters of those realms, were like movie stars to me. It was only when they matured that they became friends or counsellors, there to fill me in on the world's ways. Until then my impression was that everybody started out more or less equal, and behaved as such.

* * *

The charter landed first in Montreal, where we drove to another airport, Mirabel, an hour away. We camped out there for six hours for the much-delayed Atlantic leg. By the time we boarded, Mr. Burden and our class, twelve in all, pretty much staggered down the 747's teeny aisles, buzzing from lack of sleep and grotesque food; all sense of fun had evaporated. Elliot was sick from rye he'd pilfered from the drinks wagon, and I was humming away on anti-nausea pills that made me tired but not sleepy. Somewhere over Ireland, noises and images began to blend together, and I remember everybody's face having tweed-like dimples from the plane's seat fabric. Then, over, I suppose, France, Mr. Burden snapped to life as if for a Monday morning gym class and shouted, "Everyone up. We land in one hour."

* * *

Back to me in the hospital chair watching Jeremy sleep, wondering what he might be seeing in his dreams. I'd fallen asleep trying to guess what sort of guy he really was. Twenty is too young to be a complete adult, but most everything is there in some form or other. I didn't see track marks on his arms, or tattoos, but . . . I wondered about his childhood, and . . . I simply had no idea what to do now that he was in my life.

When the sun came up and he didn't stir, even amid the bustle of nurses, patients and machines, I left a note for him, giving him explicit directions that he was to call me once he woke up, and then I drove home. I hadn't thought about my wisdom tooth sockets in hours, but now they felt sore. For the first time in ages, my condo didn't feel simply bleak. I suppose you could say it now possessed a kind of charged bleakness.

I couldn't rest or sit down. In spite of my lack of sleep I had vast amounts of energy and began to do all those dopey metaphorical things people do when their lives are somehow new: I opened the curtains, I walked around the place with a green Glad bag pitching out old magazines, I washed the windows and floors. When I was finished, the place was so clean and orderly I thought, *I ought to have flowers in here.* So, I got in the car and drove to a place in West Van that had some cool white peonies, very late in the season, and drove back along the highway, enjoying the early afternoon of a summer day. If I'd known that sleep deprivation actually gave me energy, I'd have started depriving myself of sleep ages before. I felt great.

Then, on the other side of the highway, eight lanes over, before the Lonsdale on-ramp, I saw what I thought was a black dog walking along the highway's edge. But it wasn't. It was Jeremy, crawling westward. Oh dear God.

I slashed across three lanes of traffic and screeched to a stop on the shoulder. Leaping out of the car, I dashed across the median and four more lanes of traffic, shouting Jeremy's name. He saw me coming, smiled, waved, and kept on crawling.

"What the hell are you doing? Are you insane?"

He didn't stop, and I had to walk alongside him. He said, "I'm crawling toward the sun. To Horseshoe Bay."

"What the hell for?"

"Because it's a light, and after last night I need to follow a light."

"It's fifteen miles away—and why are you crawling?"

"It's humble."

It was a ridiculous conversation to be having. "If you want to be humble, why not just walk there with your head bowed?" I looked more closely at him; his hands and knees were torn. "Jeremy, you're cutting yourself all over." I looked at the concrete—broken pop bottles loomed. "Come on. Stop right now. The cops'll come and get you and who knows what that'll lead to." I was wondering why nobody had stopped to help him, or arrest him.

"I can watch out for myself."

"Prove it to me by stopping. Jeremy, are you high on something?"

"No, I'm not."

"Did you get my note?"

"Yup. I was going to call you at the end of my trip."

"From Horseshoe Bay?"

"It seemed to me to be a manageable goal."

I continued walking alongside him, cars ripping past us, unfazed by the sight of a plump woman and a crawling young man. "How long have you crawled so far?"

"Not too far."

"Oh God."

He looked up at me and said, "Okay, here's the deal: crawl along with me for a little while and I'll stop."

"How long is a little while?"

"From here to that hubcap up ahead."

It was about a stone's throw away. "Deal."

And thus I crawled along the Trans-Canada with my son. I've heard that parenting can strip you of dignity; here was my crash course.

He asked me, "How did you sleep last night?"

"Not much. I felt great today, though."

"I'm glad. What did you do?"

"I cleaned out my condo." A few cars honked at us, while the absence of a police presence made me wonder about the fate of civilization. "And I bought flowers. I haven't bought flowers in—well, *ever,* really."

"That's nice. What kind?"

"Peonies."

"What colour?"

"White."

"They're soft, aren't they?"

"They really are."

"I like peonies."

The cool softness of the peonies was the opposite of grit, pebbles and hot pavement.

"You've really never bought flowers for yourself before?" Despite all his spying, I managed to surprise him.

"For myself? No."

"How come?"

"Because it's like something they tell you to do in those books that try to teach you to cure loneliness. *Buy flowers for yourself because you deserve it!* I mean, a man is in a bookstore and he buys a book on loneliness—every woman in the store hits on him. A woman buys a book on loneliness and the store clears out."

"So you're lonely."

"Yes, of course I'm lonely. Who isn't lonely?" We were almost at the hubcap. "I think you're too young to understand. And there's our hubcap. Upsy-daisy."

Before I could rise, he bounced up like a Russian gymnast and reached out his hands to me. I was grateful for the lift. His hands were burning hot, and caked in blood and road grit. My hose were shot, and I'd somehow broken the heel on one shoe. I reached down and removed it.

Jeremy said, "Give me your other shoe." I did, and he broke off its heel. "There. Now you're level."

"Thank you. Let's just cross this highway without getting killed, and I'll drive toward the sun of your choice."

Inside the car, air conditioning blasting away, I felt blood surging through my carotid artery, my head thumping away. "You need to eat," I said. "I'll make you something at my place."

He was holding my peonies in his lap, looking longingly

at the sun. For the first time I let myself wonder: *Is Jeremy really nuts? Come on, Liz, be practical. You're a single woman. This is an unknown man you're letting enter your life.* I was also wondering about the depth and breadth of what appeared to be a religious streak. He certainly knew the language, and yet he didn't seem like he was the mouthpiece for any particular sect. His upbringing, I imagined. We had yet to touch on that. And of course, I had to wonder about drugs. "Are you on any medications?"

"No."

"Let me rephrase that: are you *supposed* to be taking something but you've stopped?"

"No."

"Do you like pudding?"

"Do I *what?*"

"Chocolate pudding. I only have soft foods in the apartment." I pointed to my jaw. "Wisdom teeth."

We got out of the car and quietly walked to the building's front door. The inside lobby was as cool as it had been the afternoon I returned from the exodontist. In the elevator I said, "You push the button." When we arrived on my floor, he already knew the number of my suite.

He walked around the condo, checking things out. Unlike Donna from my office, Jeremy was no faker. "I've been in three orphanages in my life, and this place is more depressing than all three combined."

"I don't care. I don't understand beauty."

"But you like the flowers, right?" He placed the peonies in the sink.

I fished around inside a bottom cupboard for something I could use as a vase. "The thing about being single," I said, “is that you never receive vases as presents. I think all single people should be issued vases by the government.”

He said, “Here.” He took a Royal Wedding cookie tin from on top of the fridge. “This is waterproof, let’s use this. I’ll trim the stems. Hold my hand.” He pulled me up. “These peonies smell nice. Like an old lady’s perfume mixed with lemon.”

He snuck one beneath my nose. I’d never noticed how peonies smell. They made me think of puffy summer clouds.

“I used to have to do the flowers at a church one of my foster families stuck me with. If I did the flowers, I could take my time and miss the talking in tongues. Not all, but most.”

He trimmed the stems with precision and speed. Before my eyes he transformed an old cookie tin and a bunch of flowers into the only truly beautiful thing my apartment had ever seen. He said, “There. You said something about food?”

My apartment seemed alive, and not ashamed of itself. Jeremy and I began to look through my cupboards and fridge, as I kept trying to sneak peeks at his face. He caught me at this and instantly knew why. “You don’t know who my father is, do you?”

“No.”

* * *

The moment we landed in Rome, my head became light and my stomach clenched like a fist. Once the group of us filtered in slow motion through Italian immigration, we sleepwalked into a European tour bus that stank of diesel,

Turkish tobacco and disinfectant. By then I was having a hard time breathing. I thought that once I was sitting down again I'd feel better, but no. Our bus was unlike any bus I'd ever taken, made in some forgotten place, like Albania. Its windows were of unlikely sizes and shapes, and its brown body was covered in brown stripes and stars. It was alien and I hated it. I instantly hated Italy or anywhere that wasn't home. The Italian roads seemed lawless and veiled in blue smoke, crammed with eggy little *parp-parp!* cars. Even the sun felt different. My sense of being somewhere other than home was overwhelming. I suspect that Europe is now one big IKEA, but back then you *knew* you were in a foreign place.

In any event, the bus promptly got stuck in a Roman traffic jam, and I started crying. Homesickness. The other kids on the bus were so spaced from jet lag they didn't even ignore me properly. They simply closed their eyes or looked out the windows maybe once every forty-seven seconds.

I caught Mr. Burden raising an eyebrow at Colleen. Colleen made a letter P for "period" using her index finger, then shrugged. Mr. Burden sighed and became almost cross. "Liz, what's up?"

I shook my head.

"I can't help you if I don't know what's bothering you."

"I want to go home."

"A bit late for that."

"I do. Now. I want to go back to the airport and get back on the plane."

"You're just nervous about being in a new country."

Again I shook my head.

"Here . . ." He reached into his coat pocket. "Take two of these."

"What are they?"

"They'll get you through the next short while."

At that point I'd have swallowed a pineapple whole if I thought it'd ease what I was feeling. From nowhere Mr. Burden produced a bottle of Orangina. I took a swig, swallowed the two pills and entered a daze that lasted fourteen hours. During it, we were marched into this bunker of a place and given a hard-boiled egg and a slice of fatty prosciutto. The boys were taken away to some other building, no idea where. When the pills finally washed out of my system, I lay on a cot—suddenly clear-headed—in the darkness of our Italian hostel. The other girls were asleep.

I felt like a prisoner of conscience. My pillow was the size of a Chiclet, the mattress as thick as a saltine cracker. I curled myself into a ball and cried quietly, doing that thing that only young people can do, namely, feeling sorry for myself. Once you're past thirty, you lose that ability; instead of feeling sorry for yourself, you turn bitter.

I'm jumping the gun. Back to that horrible little hostel with its thin-sheeted shabbiness and its aura of the ghosts of ten thousand homesick girls. Back to Italy and its striking plumbers and suddenly having to find a functioning toilet somewhere, anywhere. The hostel's toilet might as well have been a bucket. I scrambled off my mattress and walked out into the Roman night. My homesick stomach was in free fall beneath the sodium street lights that bathed the industrial nothingness with a burnt yellow tinge. There was a droning from the *autostrada* bordering the hostel's neighbourhood. This wasn't the Europe I'd been led to expect. In hindsight I can see that we'd landed in the Europe of the future.

Though I was swamped with homesickness, part of me was also enjoying a sense of inner freedom that I now know evaporates after about the age of twenty-five. It was a small joy finding an all-night gas station called Elf, maybe a few hundred yards around the corner from the hostel complex. The guys inside saw me coming from a long way away, and I could tell they were used to having girls from the hostel visit in desperation.

Okay, here's the reason we never told Mr. Burden about the gas station bathroom: its employees were the handsomest men any of us had ever seen, sculpted from gold, and with voices like songs. And there they were, in a gas station in the middle of nowhere, going to waste. They ought to have been perched on jagged lava cliffs having their hearts ripped out as sacrifices to the gods. On top of their physical blessings, these guys were charming and attentive—in both a humanitarian way and a frisky way, even charming to *me*—and . . . well . . . I'd never been flirted with before, nor has anybody flirted with me since.

They spoke their schoolboy English, with heavy Italian accents I'd always thought were a cliché: *Hello-a young-a lady. Good eve-a-ning.* All I could do was blush, and as I knew only Latin (B+) it was flummoxing to have to ask for a key, but obviously they knew what I needed, and handed it to me like a crystal champagne flute. I may have been desperate for that key, but I still dawdled; it was heaven. And best of all, the bathroom was spotless and even had a small bouquet of irises—plastic, but it's the thought that counts. When I returned to the hostel, Colleen was just waking up. I told her about the station, and she returned a half-hour later, aglow, saying how much she loved Europe.

By the end of the night, all the other girls loved Europe too. We couldn't wait for daily sightseeing to be over so we could run to the Elf station. We were awful. Nature is awful.

* * *

I said nothing, and used a dishtowel and tap water to clean my hands and knees. I'd have thought Jeremy would be crushed to not know who his father was, but he accepted it calmly. "Was it rape?"

"No."

"Incest?"

"No."

"You simply don't *know?*"

"It's more complicated than that, Jeremy. And seeing as we're both starving, let's eat first, okay?"

He pulled items from the fridge I'd barely remembered were in there. Chives. Some old cheese. A bottle of pickled something or other.

"You can cook," I said.

"Vocational school. My ticket out of hell. It doesn't matter what happens in the world, we'll always need chefs. Even during Armageddon, the troops will still need their mashed potatoes." He winked, and suddenly he was joking about themes that had so recently terrified him. After the highway incident I didn't have the energy for religious debate.

He cracked open eggs, and then whisked them with confidence, adding pinches of things along the way. Bowls and utensils came and went, and for the first time I could see the reason TV cooking shows might be watchable.

"You know, I was with Family Number Six once, and—"

"Wait—Family Number Six?"

"Yes. The sixth family I was placed with."

"Okay."

"So I was with Family Number Six visiting some hillbilly agricultural fair up north in Lac La Hache. This guy who brought our hamburgers to the table had two different-coloured eyes. So I said, 'Wow, one blue and one brown eye,' and Family Number Six froze in their seats, and remained frozen until the waiter was well out of sight. I didn't know what the big deal was, so I asked, and finally Father Number Six said, 'Don't you know what that means?' and I said, 'No,' and he said, 'It means *he's related to himself.*' Isn't that a hoot?"

"That was your *sixth* family?" I was still stuck on the number six.

He folded something into the eggs and looked heavenward, counting his family history aloud to ensure he was correct. "Six. That's right."

"How many have you had?"

"If you don't count repeats, eleven; with repeats, fourteen."

"I always pictured you as living down the street from me in a friendly suburb."

"That would have been nice. I was adopted by a family up north—moose, rifles, drunk drivers and Jesus. When I was in kindergarten, they made the mistake of telling me I was adopted, and their twins, who were a few years older than me, let me know it, too. It was bad: bruising and broken bones and a burn here or there. I ran away in grade two, and because of that I was labelled a problem child. Once that happens, you only ever move lower down the foster family food chain, until you're living in what used to be a luggage storage room owned by otherwise normal-looking serial molesters who are there merely to collect their foster care cheque from the government—which is the only reason they don't kill you, it'd cut their cash flow."

What could I say? I said, "The omelette smells wonderful. I'm going to have a small shot of Baileys to go with it. Would you like one?"

"You have anything else?"

"Not really. Wait—some of that Greek stuff—ouzo."

"That's it? How come so little?"

"Because I'm afraid of keeping booze in the house because it'll turn me into a spinster lush."

"Let's pour the Baileys into coffee. Do you have coffee?"

I did. I like coffee. I made some, topped up our mugs with the Baileys, and then we sat down to eat.

This may sound odd, but it felt like I was on a date—or rather, what I imagined a date must be like. The recognition of this temporarily froze me. My long-lost son shows up and I'm sitting there with him chatting about dog species, global warming and Mariah Carey's career arc. More to the point, I was appalled by what we weren't discussing: why he ended up being adopted in the first place, my own family history, my attempts to locate him . . . But that's what family members are for. We crave them and need them not because we have so many shared experiences to talk about but because they know precisely which subjects to avoid. Jeremy already felt like family.

We were almost done eating when the phone rang. Jeremy was closer to it and picked it up. "Liz Dunn residence."

A pause.

"Uh-huh. No, she can't talk right now."

A pause.

"Because we're having lunch. Whom shall I say called?"

A pause.

"No. As I said, we're eating lunch. I'm sure she'll phone you once we're done."

Pause.

"I'll tell her that. Goodbye." He hung up. "That was your sister."

"You shouldn't answer my phone!"

"Why not—are you ashamed of me?"

"Jeremy, chances are she's already dialed 911."

"Why?"

"You know darn well why. Because in my entire adult life nobody's ever answered my phone but me."

"You never have people here?"

"What do you think? No."

"You care what your family thinks?"

"Yes. I do. They're all I have."

"You have me now."

"I just wanted you to meet them . . ."

"Meet them how?"

"Differently." In my head I saw curtains being raised, an orchestral fanfare, flocks of dyed pigeons released on cue, and a long ramp lit by thousands of strobing flashbulbs.

Jeremy started clearing the dishes. I was immobilized by a small humming noise in my head. I sat at the table in this trancelike state and waited for Leslie to show up, which she did, maybe eight minutes later. She buzzed me from the front door and I let her in.

"Hello, Leslie."

"Lizzie, who was the man that answered your phone? You never have men here."

"Thank you, Leslie."

Holding her cellphone, she whispered, "Should I call the cops?"

I said, "Is it really that odd that I should have a man at my place?"

"Of course it is." She walked into the kitchen, expecting to see the man in my life. I followed her, but he wasn't there. I heard water noises from the bathroom.

Leslie whispered, "What's his name?"

"Jeremy."

"Jeremy? No one our age is called Jeremy."

"He's not our age."

At that moment Jeremy emerged from the bathroom, shirtless, saying, "Liz, do you have a shirt I can borrow? The one I was wearing is kind of shot." He spotted Leslie and casually said, "Hi. I'm Jeremy."

To judge from Leslie's reaction it might just as well have been a dancing Snoopy emerging from the bathroom. She took the hand he offered, saying, "I'm Leslie," in a voice that betrayed total inner confusion.

Jeremy asked, "Liz, let's have some dessert. What do you have?"

"You know the kitchen better than I do." I threw him a T-shirt from a cupboard, a HARD ROCK CAFE HONOLULU shirt William had given to me.

Jeremy looked at Leslie. "Dessert?" She nodded feebly as he slowly pulled the shirt over his head. He looked like a call boy; poor Leslie was a mess.

All we found in the kitchen was chocolate pudding in plastic tubs. Jeremy took them and began whipping them into something mousse-like and French. "So this is your sister, then?"

Leslie said, "Why do I feel like I'm dreaming?"

I said, "Leslie, there's something you need to know . . ." I watched Leslie's pupils shrink to the size of pinpricks. What an odd thing to notice at that moment. I took a glass from the counter, and the nearly empty Baileys bottle. "Drink?"

"Sure."

I poured a glass and gave it to her. "Leslie, this is my son, Jeremy. Jeremy, this is your Aunt Leslie."

Leslie sat down on a stool, and her face looked as if she had remembered where she placed something precious she'd lost many years before.

Jeremy said, "Nice to meet you." Leslie still couldn't speak, so Jeremy said, "Well, no need to let a beverage go to waste." He topped up Leslie's glass and took a sip.

Leslie looked at me, and I said, "Yup. It's true."

* * *

The day after we landed in Rome was a Sunday, and we were driven to Vatican City in our Albanian motorcoach. All I knew about the Vatican was that my dad was annoyed I'd be going there, and, well, that's about it—I still have no idea what the Pope is supposed to do. Given my limited knowledge of office politics at Landover Communication Systems, I can only imagine what a political viper's nest the Vatican must be.

Alain, the only Catholic in the class, kept his distance from us, knowing that our heretical energy might easily consume him. To paraphrase the warning he gave us before we arrived: "Religions are designed to outlive individual people, and so what looks evil and bizarre from the outside is actually just a long-term survival system."

On a practical level, the girls on the tour were ticked off that women weren't allowed to live within the City's limits, and that knowledge made our jaunt to St. Peter's Square seem like time travel. We hated it. Memory of our charming Elfs, as we called them, evaporated amid thousands of old people holding beads, looking ancient and mad. Colleen kept asking where the witch-dunking tank was. None of us felt at all remorseful about smoking outside the bus, one bus among thousands, parked on cobblestones smelling of Europe's then-omnipresent odour of diesel and urine. Mr. Burden was no narc; we puffed away. He also knew that chiding us about smoking in Europe would be about as effective as chiding us for shopping in Vancouver. Not a chance.

The boys were bored and, like us, jet lagged. The Vatican trip felt forced and dutiful. It made us wonder if Rome had the equivalent of a Playboy Mansion that was deliberately being concealed from us. We stood there like dock pilings, waiting and waiting and waiting for this little white dot of a man to come out onto a balcony and do something with his hands while his amplified voice frightened pigeons and reminded us that we were hungry and that the morning's caffe latte and croissant had long since been metabolized. The staging and the mood all served to make us feel as if we were trapped in a dying and corrupt world, one we wanted to shatter and rebuild into something better.

Back on the bus, I began to feel homesick again. It was Sunday, and the restaurant we'd been scheduled to eat in was closed, either by a strike or bad planning. The entire city, save for the Vatican, seemed to be closed. We were a dozen starving teenagers, and all we could find was a newspaper stand that sold chewing gum.

We drove past the Colosseum, but we weren't scheduled to see it for a few days yet. Mostly we drove through thousands of narrow streets designed for chariots and processions for the dead. Every shop on these streets was shuttered. I began to wonder if Italy even had an economy. That day we witnessed a sunset worth remembering, coral pink rays that fluttered above dark birds that flocked from tree to tree. It also shone over a place that actually sold food, on the highway a few miles from the hostel, on the city's outskirts. It sold hamburgers coated with Dijon mustard, which we scraped off with black plastic knives. I ate half of one, plus some more of Mr. Burden's anti-homesickness pills. By now I'd decided that I simply wanted to be under a general anaesthetic for the nine remaining days.

And thus, my second day under my belt, I once again cried myself to sleep. Boo hoo hoo. Why was I so homesick? No idea. I look back on it now and think of how visiting another country is really just the same as going into someone's house to soak up its aura. Technically, I ought to have been revelling in Italy.

Did I see many naked statues during that second day? God, yes. Everywhere. It was hard not to see them. It was even harder trying not to be *seen* seeing them. The girls cackled when confronted with stone genitalia; the boys were silent at the sight of breasts. Me, I think there's nothing erotic about female statues; as a sex we don't turn to marble well. We flourish only in paintings, whereas males in marble run the thin line between art and porn. In any event, I quickly burned out on nakedness; homesickness blotted out everything else. Unlike loneliness, it has a simple cure: going home. If only loneliness could be so easily fixed. Merely being around other humans doesn't help me—loneliness in a crowd is the most pathetic variant. On the other hand, at least in a crowd you have a chance, however slim, of meeting that cosmic person whose presence will still your fevered lonely brain. Alone in your condo, your chances are zip.

I'm doing the thing that lonely people do, which is fine-tuning my loneliness hierarchy. Which is lonelier . . . to be single and lonely, or lonely within a dead relationship? Is it totally pathetic to be single and lonely and be jealous of someone lonely inside a dead relationship? Again, remember, this is all theoretical to me. Okay, here's another one . . . is it possible to be lonely within a dead relationship while the other person isn't lonely at all? Or the corollary of that question: is it possible to be in love with two people at the same time?

When I calibrate loneliness into its own little status yardstick like this, I begin to believe I deserve what life sends me. *No, Liz, don't think like that.*

Seven years ago.

It feels like a thousand years, and it feels like yesterday.

I think I'll pour myself a glass of white wine right now.

* * *

Oh boy.

This is harder than I thought.

. . . I'm back—and I very much need to keep things in perspective here. The trip to Italy was more than twenty-five years ago. Hale-Bopp and Jeremy were seven years ago. Here I am in 2004, sitting in my condo, writing about the trip to Italy, when *BOOM!*—in the same way some people get flashes of light before a killer migraine, I have the aura that precedes a loneliness blizzard, those sweeps of loneliness that feel not just emotional but medical. Whenever I sense a blizzard about to attack, I have a few tactics I immediately employ that drain it of potency. I hop in the car, I drive to a mall or someplace filled with people, and I look at the colours of all the things on the shelves and listen to all of the voices. When the stores close, I try to find a comedy at the theatres, or I go to a coffee place. The 1990s were great because suddenly lonely people had a place where they could all be lonely together while pretending to be fine on the outside. Well, that's what *I* do in coffee shops. My head may be cyclonic with desperation on the inside, but I've worked damn hard to ensure I don't look the way I feel. I try to look as if I have a meaningful slot in society. Do people look at me, Liz Dunn, and wonder if I merit a fully stocked condo and a late-model Honda Accord? I have a job, and I'm good at it, but what if I were so messed up that I couldn't contribute to society? What if I were so messed up that I couldn't even stuff envelopes for a living? *Strap her onto the iceberg and cast her out to sea.* If it does happen someday, I'll be angry, but I won't be shocked.

* * *

Leslie can't be considered an idiot for having had no idea I was pregnant. I was a very fat and not too communicative teen, and she'd left home for college that summer after the Italian trip. When she saw me at Christmastime, I merely looked fatter than usual.

Yes, a nephew out of the blue twenty years later was a shock, but maybe not quite as big a shock as the fact that I, Liz, had done something gossip-worthy.

"Lizzie, *when? How?* How could you have been pregnant—*ever?*"

"Leslie, I may be dull, but I *am* fertile."

"How old is he?" She looked at Jeremy. "How old are you?"

"I'm twenty."

Leslie looked at me. "That's not possible. You were in high school."

"Yes. I was."

Jeremy looked at me. "Was that hard for you—having me during high school?"

"Actually, no."

Leslie barged in. "You were never pregnant in high school."

"Yes, I was."

"Who was the father?"

"Leslie, shut up already. I'm not telling you."

"Mother and Father knew you had a kid?"

"They did."

"Did William know?"

"No."

She was insulted. "They never even let on. Does Mother know about him—*now?*"

"No. You're the first. We just met yesterday."

Jeremy said, "You guys call your parents Mother and Father? That's so old-fashioned. Do you all dress like Sir Lancelot and Maid Marian, too?"

I said, "It sounds odd, but William was the first-born, and that's what he started calling them, and then it stuck with us."

Leslie was overwhelmed. "I just don't know what to say. Yes I do. Jeremy, where did you grow up—here?"

"No. All over B.C."

"Where's your family?"

"That's a tough one."

"Did you find Liz, or did she find you?"

"I found her."

I looked at Leslie and said, "Leslie, knock it off. We have plenty of time for things to unfold."

"How am I supposed to feel here, Liz?"

"Well, as this isn't really about you, I suggest you look at it as entertainment, and sit and watch the movie as it plays."

"He's twenty, Liz. And suddenly, now, you tell me you have a kid?"

"Well, you barged in here, and again, I remind you, it's not about *you*."

"How come you two met just for the first time yesterday? What happened to cause that?"

I looked at Jeremy. "It wasn't out of the blue. Jeremy was in the hospital."

"What for?"

Jeremy took the cue. "I OD'd—on some lame party drugs." He walked over and showed Leslie his bracelet.

Jeremy held the Baileys bottle upside down, hoping for a few extra drops.

Leslie was on to her third cigarette, and asked, "How long have you known about Liz—your mother?"

"A few years now."

"Why did you wait so long to introduce yourself?"

"My families have all been disasters. I tried to make it on my own, but that's not going too well. I just want to have nice, unscrewed-up family members around to make me feel normal. Without Liz, I'm going to be a write-off."

Bang! The room suddenly felt enormous—like a cathedral. And then the room grew so quiet I could almost hear Leslie's cigarette smoke swirl.

Leslie said, "That's a fair whack of responsibility to dump on one person."

"I suppose it is."

I asked Jeremy, "Where do you live? Should I be getting you home? I'm really knackered from no sleep."

"I don't have anywhere to live."

"What?"

"It's a breakup thing. Can I crash here? Just for a few days?"

"Yes. Sure. Of course you can." Instantly the chemicals in my body swirled with worry—I'd never had a guest in my place before. All I could think about were petty disruptions of my drab schedule. What was there for breakfast? I like to read my newspaper in silence. What about a key? And the bathroom!

Jeremy said, "Don't be so stressed. I'm a good guest. I'm clean. I don't steal. And I'm good at fixing things."

Leslie and I prepared a bed, cobbling together enough

blankets and pillows to make the couch sleepable. Jeremy watched all this in peace. He behaved as if I was making him happy, simply by being me. What a novel idea.

The setting sunlight turned the room a blazing orange colour, and I remember how nice it made my sheets look. Leslie was asking about dinner plans, and when I looked at Jeremy he was shivering. "Jeremy?"

Sweat was pouring from his face.

"Jeremy? What's wrong?"

"I can't see."

"You *what?*"

"I can't see."

"I don't understand you."

Leslie said, "Liz, are you sure you need this?"

"Leslie, shut up." I held him by the shoulders. "Can you see light and darkness?" I waved my hand in front of his eyes. "Anything?"

"No."

"Jeremy, what's going on here? Did you do drugs again?"

"No. Last night was an accident."

He put out his arm and I took him over to the bed we'd made. He told me he was frightened.

"Jeremy, what can I do here? Should we go to the hospital?"

"No."

"Honey, I don't know what else to do." A part of me marvelled that I'd gone from zero to "honey" inside a day.

"Call Jane. I'll give you the number."

"Who's Jane?"

"Call her. You'll find out."

He gave me a number and curled up in a fetal ball. I dialed the number, and the woman's voice on the end made me feel as if I'd caught her in the middle of her favourite TV show. "Yeah?"

"Is this Jane?"

"It is. Who's this?"

"I'm Liz."

Through the phone's receiver I could hear her posture shift. "What about him?"

"He's here at my place. He checked out of the hospital okay, and we came here to eat and now he's . . . blind."

"Oh jeez . . ."

"What's going on?"

"Give me your address. I'm coming over right now."

"What am I supposed to do? Should I call an ambulance?"

"No. Just stay there. Things'll be fine. Give me a half-hour. Okay?"

"Are you sure?"

"Trust me."

So I did.

* * *

I wish modern science would invent a drug that causes time to feel much longer, the way it felt when you were a child. What a great drug. A year would feel like a year, not ten minutes. Your adulthood would feel long and full instead of like some out-of-control carnival ride. Who would want a drug like this? Older people, I'd guess—people whose sense of passing time has hit the acceleration pedal.

And I guess they ought to also invent a drug capable of the opposite effect. Again, there'd be no immediate sensation, but after a year of the drug you'd say, *Wow! Has it been a year already? It feels like just yesterday.* Who'd take that drug? Me, when I'm lonely. And prisoners with life sentences.

Here's a third notion: what if you had to choose just *one* of these drugs? And what if taking one would instantly and forever cancel out any effect you might get from the other? I imagine most of us, myself included, would take the one that makes life feel longer. Which means that a lonely life is still better than no life at all.

I guess alcohol is the closest thing we have to a drug that makes time fly. Cocaine, perhaps? I wouldn't know about that. Maybe that's why I'm so mistrustful of booze: it makes time fly in the short term, and in the long term it obliterates memory—which is, of course, a way of erasing time.

And, okay, here's a confession: I'm a really fun drunk. Some people cry, some become belligerent and some just vanish. But me? I'm a riot. Or so my family tells me—I only ever drink with my family—God forbid I would drink at the office Christmas party.

* * *

That's my cue to continue the Italian travelogue. About four days into the trip I remained homesick and miserable, and Mr. Burden had run out of his tranquilizers. So we went to a local doctor, which sounds easy, but in Italy in the 1970s it was the equivalent in labour of filing multiple tax returns while running a triathlon. Just finding an open clinic was torture, and once we found one, we had to fill out paperwork and have it stamped. Mr. Burden lost his ability to conceal his crossness as I blubbered away in taxis that stank of mufflers. Finally we met with a pleasant young woman doctor who asked what I'd been taking, and it turns out in Italy it was an over-the-counter medication available everywhere—which was a relief, but boy oh boy, those Italians must be one highly sedated tribe. Our problem then became one of finding an open pharmacy; yet another strike or religious holiday or who knows what had closed everything down. Mr. Burden and I spent an hour in a cab, and ultimately, finding my homesickness drug ate up most of the day—our one free day, the students all exploring Rome on their own.

Once we had pills in hand, Mr. Burden gave me three, made sure I had lire and gave me directions to a restaurant where we were all going to eat a "home-cooked Italian meal" at eight o'clock. Then he abandoned me. I think he just wanted to go find a good cheese shop or a hooker.

I must say that Europe on tranquilizers is a great place. Graffiti-smothered subways felt festive; the lame and elderly animals that back then hobbled everywhere didn't bring us down; sooty buildings didn't remind you of the impending death of Mother Nature; cars parked on sidewalks, as if beached, seemed quaint. I recommend the experience.

So it was with this serenity that I arrived at the eight o'clock dinner at a large institutional restaurant that truly taxed the meaning of the term home-cooked. I was also the sole student to arrive on time. Mr. Burden was in a foul mood. He sat at a table loaded with bread sticks and plates of butter that lured wasps in through a nearby open window. A trio of elderly waiters smoked and scowled at us. I looked out the window and saw a courtyard full of bicycles, laundry and the always-present banks of tiny cars parked in happenstance mode.

"Little wretches. All of you." Mr. Burden was on his second bottle of Chianti, and I could tell he was easily going to finish it. I poured myself a glass and he just chuckled. A waiter, sniffing a tip, brought us some gnocchi in a sauce that tasted like Campbell's cream of mushroom soup. The flavour made me long for home once again. Mr. Burden, seeing sniffles begin, handed me the bottle of tranquilizers and said, "Just be careful with them." I took two. He also gave the waiter the equivalent of twenty bucks and asked for more food and wine.

And so I sat there like a Spanish infanta, quiet and happy in the knowledge that home was a mere five days away and I could remain blissed out for all 120 hours of it. I also felt grand and mature, having a solo dinner, red wine included, with a man. To Mr. Burden our dinner must have been the opposite—the low-water mark in his life. He poked at the dead food with forks as a child might poke at a slug in the garden, after which a pair of sherbet-stuffed oranges arrived, as did the other students, trickle by trickle, all apologies, all of them lying shamelessly and yet sincerely.

The big draw at dinner wasn't the food but the promise of the disco that was to follow. *Discotheque* was still a sexy word back then, newly coined. It promised sex, adventure and the chance of making out with Europeans who might even possibly resemble the singers of ABBA. Fortunately,

Mr. Burden was too drunk to much care about herding us around, and sat at the front of the bus chortling with Christy and Alain. I'd had quite a few drinks, and I was being, in my mind, quite witty. This was when the others began to notice me, but not in a *Wow-she's-cool!* way, more in a *Let's-get-the-cat-stoned* way—but how was I to know? Attention was like ambrosia to me. My behaviour became sillier, and they egged me on, mostly the boys.

Liz, I know you can dance the Hustle if you really try.

So I did, in the bus's aisle.

Liz, try this. We swiped this from the restaurant.

It was a bottle of red. I took some swigs. I was having a ball.

Liz, do you ever remove your sweater?

I did, exposing the red-and-white-checkered Levi's shirt I considered the height of style.

The disco was a big laundry room with a glitter ball, seven coloured light bulbs and that strange Euromusic—like normal music but with, of all things, an oompah band in the background. There was one other youth group there, from Austria. We mingled, marvelling at revelations such as that Vienna had Kentucky Fried Chickens and that, as a currency, the lira, with all its zeroes, was silly to them too. And I danced, *oh* did I dance. I shudder to think of what I must have looked like.

After an hour, about seven of us went up to the roof to smoke, or, rather, six people did, and I was the seventh, happy that people weren't brushing me off. The night air was damp and smelled like an uncleaned fridge. It began to rain and we all pretended not to notice our collective shivering while we huddled under a ledge.

The Colosseum was surprisingly close, and to my drunken eyes seemed like a backdrop for a Bugs Bunny cartoon rather than an arena in which history was created. An afternoon slave killing? Quite jolly, I thought. Did they have guys selling the Roman equivalent of beer and hot dogs? The Austrians gave me a swig from their red wine bottle, and I remember feeling dizzy and wanting to leave the group. I went behind a ventilation unit, where I listened to the acid rain dissolving the city, atom by atom. I developed walking bedspins, and then . . . ? There lies the question mark.

The next thing I remember is being packed away into the bus headed to the hostel, everybody looking absolutely dreadful. Mr. Burden was tanked, and I had my face stuck in a plastic bag from a Standa department store. Once back in our hostel, those girls who weren't in too rough shape walked down the road to use the toilet and to flirt—at nearly two in the morning—with the golden Elf men. Tramps. I'd have happily joined them had I not felt like a swiftly revolving sludge pool.

As for the remaining 110 hours or so, our Roman tour became textbook dull. Our debauched night out had left everyone hungover and surprisingly mousy. I take it on faith that we saw the Trevi Fountain, the Pantheon's dome, a hundred fountains and an equal number of churches, churches, churches, and more churches still. Few memories remain. Only a side trip to the ruins at Ostia Antica made any deep impression on me—the excavated ruins of a typical Roman day, allowing us to imagine the day-to-day world of the ancients. As I think about it, this is what my apartment reminded me of when I returned from my wisdom tooth surgery: a place in need of thawing or excavation to somehow bring it to life or meaning.

Rome—what else? The cracked travertine floors of museums, neon signs advertising Candy appliances, and elaborately naked statues on every corner. Oh—and there were streets named after famous dates, like Via XX Settembre. I began to think about human civilization—no better place to do so than in Rome—and I wondered what would happen if life just kept on going, on and on, and how, in a thousand years, every day of the year would have its own street named after it, and they'd be into repeats. Why, I wondered, didn't North America have streets named after dates?

In 2004, I no longer wonder.

* * *

Our homeward flight seemed to pass in all of three seconds, and once at the Vancouver airport my homesickness vanished as though it had never been. My parents met me, and I squeaked with delight upon seeing them. Father's sole question to me at the luggage carousel was, "So, how was your time travelling back to the past?" My mother shushed him, and on the ride home they filled me in on Leslie's job hijinks back east. I may have just been to Italy, but she was the interesting one.

There's not much more to say here except for two confessions. The first confession I tell you only because it helps explain the second. My first confession is that I'm fat. I've said that I was fat as a child, but I remain fat as a woman.

There. Perhaps you might not wish me to go any further. Who wants to know about a fat person's life or what goes on in her mind? Surely my words must unconsciously ooze the stuff. Even[lard]when[carbs]I[calories]try[sugar]concealing[pig]it, [pork]I[cholesterol]speak[celery]like[cottage cheese]a[tuna]fatty. Big deal.

Even in the car riding home from the airport, I knew that Leslie's exploits would eclipse my own. I'm realistic. I have no problem being me, except that I'm lonely. I've lost a few pounds in recent years—better proteins, more fruit and all of that—but when you've spent four decades being fat, even were I to become a stick figure, I'd still be fat in my head. Guys would just *know. I*'d know.

And you've probably guessed the second confession, which is what happened nine months later. I'm not going to pretend this was some cosmic virgin birth. When I skipped my first few periods, I just assumed that it sometimes happens when nature begins to toss all these new and marvellous changes at you. After about the fifth month I thought, *Okay—there's something going on here.* Then I spent a month thinking about that, which was really just denial. By the sixth month I could feel junior doing somersaults and kicks, and basically, I was too scared to tell my parents—specifically, Mother.

I've not discussed my mother much. She's not a mean person, but her moods have always been both extreme and random. Today she takes something nice twice a day, and she's stable—still random, but the mood yo-yos are gone. Back then? When she lost it, dogs halfway across the mountain bayed and yowled in sympathy. The moment they were old enough, William and Leslie landed summer jobs as far away as possible. Being with Mother all day long for the entire summer? Unthinkable. Unfortunately, two unsuccessful stabs at summer camp—homesickness again—ruled me out for that sort of gig. I suppose it's a major reason for breaking into the houses of strangers: a house with no possibility of relatives walking into the room and going random on me. People coming home unbeknownst to me were nothing compared with this.

The best thing about being young is being stupid. Or rather, the best thing about being young is being too stupid to know how stupid you really are. By the seventh month, just as school ended, I was tired a good deal of the time. Mother briefly floated the idea of mono, until she remembered it was a kissing disease. Luckily, my morning sickness had been brief enough to be passed off as flu, even to myself.

As the baby grew, I don't think I once thought of it as something I could keep. Many women moon and wonder about their expected baby's little fingers and downy hair. Me, I was trying to figure out how to have it and leave it in a milk crate on the steps of the church where Taylor Way meets the highway. Dumb as it sounds, I was hoping for early morning contractions, which would allow me to go out into the municipal watershed forest, have the baby, and then drop it off at the church and get home in time for dinner.

You wish.

Tuesday in late August was when the contractions came. Father was upstairs with his ham radio, and Mother and I were watching TV. From nowhere I had a cramp like never before—seismic. Mother looked at me and said, "What? What's going on?"

"It's a cramp."

"Some cramp."

"Mmm." I was trying to play it cool so I could go fetch the birthing kit I'd assembled: blankets, soda water, Aspirin and feminine products, all of them bundled into a yellow Dairyland milk crate along with a clean blanket placed in a plastic bag, which I'd planned to wrap the baby in before placing it on the church's stoop.

"What have you been eating?"

"Nothing. Just dinner. And some strawberries."

"Local strawberries?"

"Yeah. The girl in the berry van down at the corner gave me some."

"They water those things with raw sewage."

"They do *not.*"

"Don't go blaming me and my dinner for your cramps."

"Was I blaming you?"

We went back to TV. I was about to slip out when the next cramp came with a good kick. I felt like I'd run into a tree on my bike. There was no way I was going out into the forest to have the baby. What had I been thinking?

"Strawberries. You had to eat them unwashed."

"Take me to the hospital."

She turned toward me. I'm not an alarmist, nor am I a fibber. So she couldn't ignore this. "Okay. I will."

The drive there was tense. Father was clueless, but Mother knew something was going on. "Lizzie, there's something you're not telling me."

"Later, Mother." The thought of a shit fit in the car was too much to deal with. She probed all the way to the hospital, but I was offhand. I'd gone this far—I might as well go the whole way.

It was a slow night, and this was back when hospitals were better funded and better staffed than now. They took me into one of their unoccupied slots (just two over from where I'd meet Jeremy so many years later), and they asked me routine questions, Mother repeating the words "Unwashed strawberries" to whoever was nearby. The duty doctor came in, said hello, asked a few questions, poked around a bit and said, "Get her up to maternity. Now."

I shrugged as they wheeled me away.

Mother's face!

* * *

In the half-hour between my phoning Jane and her arrival, Jeremy was untalkative. Leslie and I were baffled. We both suspected it was drugs, and all we could do was wait. Then he said, "I can see out of my left eye now. And it's not drugs."

"What is it?"

"I—don't want to say what it is. I won't say the words."

"Why not?"

"Jane will be here soon."

We sat in the living room amid stacks of sad videos, drinking coffee and waiting.

Then the mysterious Jane arrived. I'd been half expecting a dominatrix or a Goth with unshaved armpits, but instead I opened my door to a sensible-looking woman, twentyish, long face, a nice smile and a blue anorak. If she were to own a dog, it would be a collie with an IQ of 115; she might have been canvassing for the SPCA.

"I'm Jane."

"Liz."

"Where is he?"

"In there."

I was relieved. She sat down beside Jeremy and touched his face. He placed his hand on hers and said, "I'm sorry."

"Shush."

Jeremy fell asleep as if hypnotized on a stage before an audience. I asked, quite frantically, what was wrong with him, but Jane instead questioned me as to how Jeremy and I had connected, and how he'd ended up at my place. Once she was satisfied that I was both genuine and concerned, she said, "MS."

"Oh."

"You don't really know what it is, do you?"

"Nobody ever does."

Leslie said, "Like that Stephen Hawking guy—the smartest guy on earth."

"No, that's something else. This is multiple sclerosis."

I said, "It's bad—isn't it?"

Jane nodded. "It is."

"How bad?" asked Leslie.

Jane asked, "Can I have a cup of coffee?"

I poured her one.

At first none of us knew where to start, and then things became very medical very quickly. For the sake of brevity I'll say that, just like Rome, MS has many websites.

In capsule form: For unknown reasons, myelin sheaths that protect the brain and spinal cord's nerve cells are attacked and dissolve, bit by bit. Some people blame dietary wheat. Some blame mercury amalgam fillings. Some blame viruses deposited in freshwater lakes visited by migrating ducks. Regardless, the lesions of MS rob a victim of body functions in random sequence: balance, heat sensation, clear thinking and stamina—and everything else. In the end the body loses the battle.

Jane said, "It typically hits people in their twenties and early thirties, but it can skew either way. There's no cure, there are a few palliative measures that can be taken, and that's basically it."

"Nothing?"

Jane said, "Nothing. Fewer men get MS than women, but men get hit harder. Jeremy has Progressive MS. Most people have Relapsing Remitting MS. His body is unknitting itself."

We were quiet. I said, "Jeremy said the two of you had broken up."

"We did."

Another highly freighted lull here, the freight being, *What sort of monster would dump a guy with MS?*

"Look," Jane said, "I know what you're thinking. The reason we split is because he was doing drugs. Even if he didn't have MS, I'd have dumped him."

Leslie, who did heaven knows how many drugs with her husband, kept a studiously neutral look on her face. I said, "I can understand."

"No, you see, every time he does them, it accelerates his MS. He's on fast-forward with this stupid disease. And with these new chemicals out there—I mean—they turn your brain into a dying coral reef. If he's not going to watch out for himself, then I'm not going to be the one being a babysitter and martyr for the guy. We've talked this through a hundred times."

I asked, "Why does he say he takes drugs?"

"To forget he has MS."

We needed to change the topic, and Jane and Leslie both wanted to know more about my meeting with Jeremy. I suppose they wanted syrup and violins, but I didn't give them that. I told them about the phone call, the doctor and the flowers—but not about crawling down the highway. "Look, he'd already known me for years, so I can't have been too new a subject for him."

"But for you? How did you *feel?*"

Their eyes drilled into me.

What *about* me?

There'd been no real digestion time that day, and the news just kept on coming. "I really don't know."

Jane asked, "Who was his father?"

"I can't tell you," I said.

"How come?" Leslie asked. She was quite cross that I was still holding out.

"I'm not telling anybody until I tell Jeremy."

Strangely enough, we then discussed wisdom teeth. It was neutral yet medical; timely yet irrelevant.

Jeremy made a noise. "Mom?"

I can't tell you how good the word *Mom* made me feel.

"Can I stay here tonight? I'll sleep on the couch."

"It's fine by me, but maybe Jane wants you back wherever you live."

"On Commercial Drive. In a fifties apartment building. Jane won't want me. I really blew it this time."

Jane made a face.

"Why'd you do drugs if you know it's going to make things worse?"

"Because after I come down, I can see things I couldn't see before."

"Like the sun over Horseshoe Bay fifteen miles away."

"Please don't get mad at me. But I did—see the sun, and it wasn't the sun we usually see. It was different."

Jane said, "I have to go."

"Jane—"

"Come by and get your stuff tomorrow."

As soon as she was gone, I asked Jeremy how long his visions had been going on; Jane hadn't mentioned that.

"Just over a year now. I was at a party and I froze. I mean, I was locked inside my body, but I might just as well have been concrete. It scared the crap out of me."

"How long were you frozen?"

"Only two minutes. When Jane and a few other people dragged me out of the dance area, it was like I was a plank. We were all scared. We chalked it up to the drugs I wasn't supposed to be doing, but which I was."

"When did you start—seeing things?"

"Maybe a month later."

Leslie's phone rang. It was her husband, Mike. "Liz, I have to go. There's going to have to be a huge family mob scene dinner or something like that. You know it, right?"

"Can we delay it a little?"

"We'll talk tomorrow. When are you going to call Mother and tell her?"

"When Jeremy's asleep."

"She'll flip."

* * *

Oh, to have a photo of Mother's face when they wheeled me up to maternity! Or Father's—or, for that matter, mine. They looked as though they'd just been pelted with eggs.

Did they ever let on to the staff that they didn't know? No. Once again, the good thing about families is that everybody knows exactly when not to discuss something big.

The birth wasn't painful—I think I'm a born procreator. I've had pimples more painful than childbirth. I exaggerate, but that part of things was easy, even more so with the drugs they gave me. What I recall more than anything is being embarrassed at having so many people focus their attention on me: *Look at someone else! Everybody stop staring at me!* I don't like people making a fuss over me, childbirth or not. Nurses kept on wanting to hold my hand, which seemed corny to me, but then I realized I'd never held anyone's hand before, and this made me sad—which was again interpreted as something medically wrong, but no, it was simply me being sad for a moment.

I could hear Mother out in the hallway yelling at a matron, and an orderly not allowing her or Father entry into the theatre. If Mother had played her cards right and hadn't had a mood see-saw, she could have been right there with me. It was a relief to have them out of the way, but I'd have to face them soon enough. I wished the nurse would jab Mother with a needle—*I* was the one supposed to be doing the screaming.

The proceedings became heavy-duty: bright lights, green smocks, stainless steel tools that performed tasks best left unknown. I thought of that night on the disco roof, rain and all, and the Austrian boys and their red wine. *Well, they were at least quite handsome, so maybe this kid will get a good break out of life.*

And then out popped my son, chubby and pink and covered with muck. *I made that—I did something useful, I did.* A moment after the birth, they asked me if I wanted to hold him, and this is when I overrode the effect of the drugs, the craziness of the surprise, the screaming mother, the aerospace maternity technology; I thought about what I knew would happen to this child, how it didn't stand a chance if it was saddled with me as a mother, or with my parents in the picture, and with—oh, forget about it. There was no chance this kid could stay with me, and I knew it. Life had already taught me not to want what I can't have. I said no, I didn't want to hold the baby. Not even for a second. We never even made eye contact—I wouldn't allow myself—and so they whisked him away, and with him a whole other way of life was gone forever. Me? They pretty much gave me an Aspirin, a bowl of tapioca and, after one day, a discharge. Jeremy stayed there for light treatment to correct a slight anemia.

Afterwards, life at home was grim at best. Father had no idea what to say or do. Mother? Thank heaven for Valium. I hammed up the too-tired-to-talk aspect of the birth, and Mother hopped like a bird between my room and the TV room down the hall, sleepless and restless.

"It was Rome. I know it was Rome. What happened there?"

"Nothing happened there, Mother."

"It was nine months ago. How stupid do you take me to be?"

Of course I eventually told her what I thought had happened, but what could they do about it? Call the school and demand compensation or justice—and, in doing so, reveal that they hadn't even known I was pregnant, possibly inviting a squad of social agencies onto the front doorstep to question their viability as parents? One of Mother's many moods was paranoia. In this case it worked to my advantage. For the months leading up to the birth, and in the days following it, I played out in my head all possible what-to-do-with-the-baby scenarios, and in all of them Mother came out looking bad. Adoption was the least harmful scenario. I said, "Hospitals must have closets full of adoption papers. I'll ring and ask for one."

As for my baby, I did look at him once in the nursery while he slept in his see-through light box, and he was beautiful. I thought of those handsome Austrians on the roof, and was sure they were all good genetic raw material. Nature can be cunning that way.

And my heart did go out to my son, but I placed my faith in the provincial adoption system, that it would give him a family as bland and middle-class as my own—or perhaps protect him from families as bland and middle-class as my own. I offloaded my guilt onto bureaucracy—with hindsight, a stupid and childish thing to do. That's what I blame myself for. Not the rest.

* * *

I was enjoying the relative peace now that Leslie and Jane had left. Leslie was no doubt on her cellphone, blanketing the airwaves with gossip, and my phone would shortly be ringing—Mother.

Jeremy stirred, as if having a bad dream. Then his eyes opened, and even with just the hallway light shining on us, I could tell he could see again.

"What is it, Jeremy?"

"Farmers."

"What about farmers?"

"I had this vision."

"You mean a dream?"

"No. Dreams are boring. I had a vision. I told you I have them. It was these farmers, out in the Prairies, growing wheat or something, and it was spring, but they weren't planting their fields. They were standing out in the middle of those rural roads that go right to the horizon, and it was midday, and they were looking up at the sun shining through an all-black sky."

"Why were they doing that?"

"They were hoping they'd see something there."

"What?"

"Further instructions on what to do. I think they believed that the world was to end that year—that's why they didn't bother sowing their seeds. And they weren't crazy or anything. They accepted the end times as a given, and weren't fighting the idea."

"Were there any farmers' wives in this vision? They might have a different view of it."

"They believed too. They were on their porches, throwing their jarred preserves into their yards—beets and beans and tomatoes—with the glass shards like coins in the sun, and the juices trickling into the soil, which was all chalky and grey, and the juices were feeding the things sleeping inside it—worms and embryos of locusts."

"Okay then, did the farmers get any information from the sky?"

"They did."

"What was that?"

"They were told the world is a place filled only with sorrow, and that people have no idea where it is we're destined for. Disaster is inevitable, whether it be by our own doing or as an act of God. That's why they shouldn't be afraid—because the end is going to happen no matter what."

"This made the farmers feel better?"

"Yeah, it did. They were also told that there was a gift awaiting them, and that shortly they'd be given a signal—I don't know what the signal was to be—and that they'd receive this gift."

The farmers' plight chilled me. It seemed to echo my own plight in a way Jeremy didn't realize, but I didn't let on about this. "How do you feel about it? You, personally."

Jeremy relaxed. "I wish I could say the things I see are crap, but I just don't know. Why would my own life become so messed up like this with MS if there wasn't some sort of compensation?"

"I don't always think life hands out compensations, Jeremy."

"What about life after death?"

"What about death after life after death?" It sounded clever, but I wasn't completely sure what I meant by it. A bad joke.

"So you don't believe in infinity?"

"What a funny question. No. Infinity is a mathematical parlour trick. It's artificial. It didn't even exist until recently."

Jeremy smiled. "My brain hurts."

I tapped him lightly on the knee and said, "Brains can't hurt. They don't have nerves. I'm not joining your pity party."

"Aren't you a tough nut? I bet you laughed when Bambi's mother got shot."

I lost it completely. I couldn't remember the last time I'd laughed so hard.

"What's so funny? What's so funny?"

I picked up my *Bambi* video from the coffee table and told him about my visit from the lovely Donna of Landover Communication Systems, our patron saint of weak coffee and terse notes on the lunchroom fridge asking staff not to touch carrot and celery sticks belonging to other people. Jeremy saw the humour, and said, "Your mother's going to freak when she finds out about me."

"Well, yes." Leslie had forgotten a pack of cigarettes on the table. I lit one, and then, on cue, the phone rang.

It was Mother. She didn't even say hello, instead merely shouting, "Is it true?"

"Is *what* true, Mother?"

"I'll be right there."

"Thank you, Mother." I hung up and went to the kitchen. "I'm making coffee. Do you want any? Are you allowed to drink it?"

"Yes and no. How much does your mother know about—I don't know . . . *me?*"

"You'd be amazed how little."

"Start."

"It's just not as easy as that."

"Why not?"

"Just hang on awhile. If you waited for four years, you can wait a bit longer."

We shortly heard four (always four) demanding knocks on my door, the downstairs buzzer somehow bypassed.

Once I opened the door, I saw her eyes bulging, but I could tell by musculature alone that she'd taken her meds.

"Mother, come in."

She hesitated.

"No, really. Come in."

"I didn't think this would ever happen," she said.

"I didn't either, Mother."

"The adoption people told us he was beyond access."

"Yes, they did."

"It's not my fault. It never was."

"Nobody's saying it is."

Mother remained outside until I really insisted she step in. She suddenly seemed so old, her steps assisted by an invisible aluminum walker as she gently stumped into the living room. There she found Jeremy standing up by the coffee table. She looked at him and said, "So it really is you."

Jeremy said, "It sure is."

"Come over to me," she demanded, and Jeremy did. You'd think the woman was selecting melons at Super Valu. "I wish my husband could have been here to meet you. You look a bit like him. He was killed in a car wreck some years ago. In Hawaii."

"I know. Please. Sit down."

"No. I want to look at you a second." She circled Jeremy, surveying him from all angles. This clearly made him uncomfortable. She said, "There's your father in there, Lizzie—can you see him?"

"A bit."

Jeremy said, "Please. Sit down."

I said, "Do you want some coffee?"

"Do you have any of that Baileys left?"

"All out."

"Then no thank you." She looked at Jeremy. "So where did you grow up, then—Vancouver?"

"No. In the sticks. All over the place."

"Oh—was your family military?"

"I wish. And it was families *plural*. Eleven, all told, and always within B.C."

"Eleven?"

"Yup."

Mother looked at Jeremy as if he'd been marked with a thirty percent discount, but he ignored this. "Most of my families were religious. Whenever something went wrong, religion always surfaced during my interviews with Social Services, and they always thought a different religious family out in the boonies could fix me."

"It's not like you needed fixing," I said.

"No. I could have told Social Services about being chained to the laundry pole for sixteen hours during bear season. But my foster mom would have raised one eyebrow, looked skyward and said, 'Kids. The imaginations they have.'"

Mother said, "Oh. Well, I only wanted to know where you were raised."

"Now you know," I said.

"When did you two meet? How?"

"I contacted Liz."

"We were always told it was impossible to find you."

"It is, unless—"

I interrupted. "Jeremy found a loophole in the system."

Mother said, "I've thrown thousands of dollars at the system for years, and I could never find out anything."

"You *what?*"

"I pray in a closet for him. I haven't had a proper night's sleep since the day we signed the papers."

"Why didn't you tell me?"

"We never talked about him—*you*—Jeremy. Ever."

Jeremy said, "I insist—you two need coffee."

Mother began speaking like she was talking in her sleep. "I've also thought about you during the days, too. Usually it's when I'm preparing dinner, and in my head I'm wondering how many portions to make. I'm at the sink peeling potatoes, or maybe it's while I'm ironing a shirt. Don't ask why. I'm standing up and doing something dull with my hands. Leslie and William have kids, but for some reason it's you I've missed. You were the first. I worry about Leslie's kids, but when I think about them, I've never pulled over to the side of a road, out of the blue, feeling like I've been kicked in the chest."

A bit of my wind had left me. "I don't think I can take any more emotion here."

Mother ignored me. "Leslie says you're sick. That you called Liz from the hospital."

"In a sense."

"You look fine. What's wrong with you?"

I said, "Multiple sclerosis."

"Oh."

I tell you, those two words are charged, yet nobody knows with what. Perhaps bones darkening and shattering; bruises that come and go without reason, or skin feeling stung by a bee, the skin then wasting away, even while in bed. The dreaded wheelchair, or a plastic bubble, and doubtless dozens of brown plastic medication bottles. I don't know. Even now that I know what the beast is, it still makes no sense to me.

Seeing us both standing there at a loss for words, Jeremy had mercy on us and launched into a brief description of the disease. Mother bit her lips; afterwards she asked Jeremy how he was feeling right then.

"Okay. I had a nap."

"He's going to be staying here tonight."

Mother said, "Here? Why would anyone want to stay here?"

"*Thank you,* Mother."

Jeremy said, "I'm sleeping on the couch."

"No you're not. You'll come stay at the house with me. I have two perfectly good guest rooms, and one has an ensuite bathroom. And I just made Nanaimo bars, too."

"Nanaimo bars? You drive a hard bargain, Mrs. Dunn, but no, I want to stay here with Liz."

The sun had gone down, and the sky was a dazzling deep blue. I said, "Mother, let's just let Jeremy sleep. Jeremy . . . ?"

Jeremy had started to tremor slightly, as if his whole body was stuttering. We helped him out of his trousers, leaving him in his underwear and a T-shirt. He quickly fell asleep.

He was a beautiful boy, and Mother and I stood there watching him as if he were a painting. I was unsure of whether I could make any artistic claim to having created him. He was the wonderful Christmas present, and I was merely the box, the wrapping paper and the postage stamp. He opened his eyes briefly at one point, but unwarranted attention clearly didn't seem strange to him, and he fell asleep once more.

I was bagged. For the time being, the old pattern of silence Mother and I shared would remain in place. We had a quick hug and agreed to meet again the next day.

After she left, I walked around switching off the condo's lights. *This must be what it feels like to be a normal person at the end of a day: small and large dramas; secrets and revelations; coffee cups and plates caked with dried food.* With just the stove light on, I sat on a kitchen chair and gazed at the sleeping form on the couch. Was it really just days ago that I believed this room to be incapable of life?

Jeremy's body twitched like a perch on a dock.

"Jeremy, are you okay?"

"I don't know."

I walked over and sat beside the couch. "Bad dream?"

"Dream? No. Not at all. It was the farmers I saw earlier."

"Oh. Okay. What happened?"

"If I tell you, you'll keep it between us, right?"

"Yes—but can I ask you first, real quick, how you know the difference between a dream and a vision?"

"That's easy. When I see something, I'm really *there*. It's like in the movies, when a character travels back in time, everybody thinks he's crazy, and then he pulls a ring or something out of his pocket, and everybody suddenly realizes he was telling the truth and truly *was* back in time. It's that feeling."

"Okay. What about the farmers?"

"They were still out on the road, wearing their dungarees and looking at the sky and waiting to be told something more. I could tell they felt cheated, and I could tell they were confused and probably angry. Then they heard a voice from just over a hill. It was a woman's voice, and as

I heard it I thought how voices in visions are only supposed to come to people like Joan of Arc burning at the stake, assisted by angels, but instead this voice was like the woman at the end of the 1-800 number you call to order stuff off of TV."

"What did she say?"

"She said she had news that the farmers wouldn't like. She said that the farmers were unable to tell the difference between being awake and being asleep."

"Like we've just been talking about?"

"I don't know about that. But the woman's voice told them that the farmers had lost their belief in the possibility of changing the world. They asked her what she meant by that, and she said that the farmers just assumed that the lives of their children or grandchildren would be identical to their own lives, that there wouldn't or couldn't be any difference."

"It sounds like they had to choose between certainty and peace."

"Kind of. I guess what was weird was that the farmers had no trouble with this. They said, 'Okay.' And so the voice told them that this was foolish, and because of this there had to be a change of plans."

"Uh-oh."

"They were told that death without the possibility of changing the world was the same as a life that never was. The voice said that they'd soon hear words that would make them believe again in a future."

There was a silence. I said, "That was really crazy and scary what you were doing today, out on the highway."

"Sorry. But when I get in that state, I can't stop myself. I really need some sleep."

"Good night, Jeremy."
"G'night."
What was I to make of this strange young man?

* * *

In the few remaining weeks of summer following Jeremy's birth, Mother and I weren't enemies, but we weren't friends.

To our mutual satisfaction, in the local shopper paper Mother found a divorcee named Althea down near the ocean who gave painting lessons from her basement. She was an aging, scatterbrained, shawl-wearing fertility goddess. Her students, all of whom were far older than me—and all emotional disasters—showed up at eleven each morning, and we painted still lifes composed of Althea's bottles from the night before. Around two, once Althea's gin headache faded, we took our canvas boards to the sun-baked rocks around Lighthouse Park, where we painted arbutus trees, salt- and wind-warped cedars, the calm August ocean and maybe a few rogue clouds. We sat in tribal clusters, and as it was the seventies I had all of these damaged adults around me spilling their guts about multiple orgasms, erectile dysfunction and cocaine abuse. I could barely control my palette knife while a modelling ingenue confided about how much sex and cocaine she'd had the weekend before, and how it "fatigued" her, "but you know, cocaine is non-addictive—" All of those seventies lies. My paintings were dreck, sold at a garage sale ages ago, and doubtless some smart-aleck youngster has found them for sale in Salvation Army thrift stores and has now hung them up as cheesy ironic monstrosities—which is what they were.

My parents and I obviously never told William or Leslie about the baby. It was simply easier not to. My role in the family was to be the maiden aunt, the dutiful one who milks the cows and feeds the chickens; having a child wasn't in the script we'd all been handed.

The good thing about Mother being erratic is that when her behaviour became even wilder after the birth, William and Leslie just thought it was a bad patch and gave it no more consideration.

Father threw himself into his job at the engineering firm and was gone much of the time. Around me he was quiet, but no more quiet than usual. He gave the occasional sigh, but I think he mended from the experience quickly. Mother, though, had nobody in her life to speak with, and she stewed about the birth far more than I did. Teenagers can be mean and oblivious, and I was no different in that regard. It didn't occur to me that Mother would be undergoing something major. I now cringe at my callousness, but what's done is done.

* * *

Oh—before I forget, my mother never knew about the cluster of abortions that occurred in the few months after the Italian trip. It was common lore at the school, even for outsiders like me: those girls sauntering off to the Elf station brought back souvenirs, four in all. I still have a photo of the Elfs, who probably have offspring circling the globe. I took the photo the day before we left. The bus crapped out on us and we were marooned at the hostel, so we all went over for a group shot. The photo is yellowed, and you can sense the stinking, noisy *autostrada* just to the side of the station, and you can see something in the eyes of the girls. They'd changed.

* * *

After Jeremy fell asleep again that first night, he woke up sweating into his second hour. I'm not sure if he even knew it was me, but he said, "The women on the porches! Oh! Suddenly they're far more beautiful than they were before. They're in white dressing gowns. There are flowers in vases on porch railings and in their hair—shasta daisies and bachelor's buttons. These beautiful women are asking the voice what it was they're supposed to do next."

"What is it?"

"They're told to believe that we're all sick in our own way—and that life is work—and rewards often seem more accidental than based on merit. And they're told about the delay, and that they won't be receiving their gift—not that year—they have to make it through the winter first."

"And?"

"The voice stops there. The men and women are frightened. It's too late to plant seeds. Their stored foods have been destroyed. They know winter will soon arrive, and they don't know what to do."

Jeremy paused, then fell asleep once more.

* * *

It's an axiom of family life that children in their late teens yearn to meet and befriend aunts, uncles and cousins across the country, relatives of whom little has been said over the years, and whose presence throughout their life has been fleeting. *I bet Mom and Dad never gave so-and-so a chance. I'll be the one who discovers their unmined charms, and I'll be the one who uses my spunk to knit the family closer together.*

The newly discovered aunts, uncles and cousins are then revealed to be just like our immediate family, except funnier and more charming and less disciplinary. They inflate our sense of adulthood.

And then the years pass, and with them the ease and confidence around the new-found relatives. Intractable personality problems emerge and tempers flare. Chances are that you, yourself, are turning into one of your parents—the exact people your relatives chose to avoid in the first place. It all turns into a mess, which is fine; families are messy.

I mention this because that's the way it started with Jeremy. He was an undiscussed relative living far away who showed up on my doorstep one afternoon. Of course I wanted him to be witty and smart and wonderful, but Jeremy, to his credit, never tried to see me as perfection embodied. Which is probably why I liked him so much. And he'd been, if not spying, keeping his eye on me for all that time before we met. My life couldn't have surprised him in any way.

On Jeremy's first morning in my place, I woke up to the smell of breakfast in the air. I sat bolt upright: eggs, butter, salt and oil and a touch of chives were like tendrils from under the crack of my bedroom door. I threw on my terry cloth housecoat and poked my head out into the hallway to the kitchen. Jeremy, fresh as a Gap clerk, asked, "Do you like your omelettes chunky or *baveuse?*"

"What's *baveuse?*"

"Runny."

"*Baveuse,* please."

In my bathroom mirror, my cheeks had only slight yellow bruising, and the swelling was down, if not gone. And there was *another person* in my apartment. Cooking eggs. He was family, but he . . . I'd never had anybody spend a night in my apartment. I began to wonder about practical things like the bathroom and whether its contents sent out bad signals. Not stupid things like women's products, but whether or not it seemed like a *real person's* bathroom. Whimsical bathroom gadgetry is so embarrassing; dried-out starfish and sponges make me worry about extinction; all-white tile bathrooms remind me of the hostel bathroom in Italy.

I inspected my surroundings, both architecturally and biologically. Odours? Stains? Discolorations? Failures of imagination?

When I finally went into the kitchen, Jeremy said, "Mornings are the best time for me. My body rarely turns freaky until the afternoon, so I try to do what I can as quickly as I can."

"You didn't have to cook breakfast."

"Being useful has always kept me safe."

"That's how I feel."

"You do?" One lip of pale yellow egg was being folded on top of another; he must have beaten extra egg whites into the mix.

I said, "Unless I contribute to society, I pretty much figure they'll scoop me up in the middle of the night and toss my condo and job and bank account to people who are more deserving than me."

"How long have you thought that?"

"It's not thinking; it's a feeling. Ever since I can remember."

He handed me the omelette, which was thick like a pancake but full of air, too. It deflated when I forked it.

Jeremy asked if I liked my work.

"I think big companies are like marching bands. You know the big secret about marching bands, don't you?"

"No. What is it?"

"Even if half the band is playing random notes, it still sounds kind of like music. The concealment of failure is built right into them. It's like the piano—as long as you play only the black keys, not the white ones, it'll sound okay, but on the other hand it'll never sound like real music either."

"How's your omelette?"

"Good." From the kitchen table I glanced at the living room. It was spotless. "Jesus, Jeremy, you didn't have to clean the whole place."

"I noticed that there are no family photos anywhere in your place, not even on your fridge."

"I've always meant to put some up."

"Sometimes when I'd stay with one family for long enough to make friends, I'd go to my friends' houses, look at their family photos, and it was so strange, seeing the same people, always in the same kind of photos, but growing older together. I only have maybe three photos of me before the age of twenty. School pictures."

"You were a beautiful baby. Even I could tell that the moment you were born."

The compliment was lost on him. "I used to steal family

pictures from my friends," he said. "Smaller ones that they'd never miss. Those pictures and my clothes were the only things I ever took from one placement to the next. My plan was that when I finally escaped the system I could hang up all of these photos on my walls, and girls would look at them and think it was great that I had a family, and that I liked my family."

"Smooth."

"I've always liked those super-healthy girls who smell like freshly mown lawns—the ones who secretly want to make love to chestnut-coloured horses named Thunder. All of my stepsisters had mall hair, and if they tried to make it with me and I said no, they'd blame me for eating the leftover Kentucky Fried Chicken in the fridge, even though they were the ones who did it. When you're in foster care, even something dumb like that can make them trade you in."

I finished eating and lit a cigarette. "I look like hell."

"So?"

"Point well taken. You know what?"

"What?"

"Let's go shopping for a fold-out bed this morning."

"That's a good idea."

* * *

Soon we were in my Honda driving to Park Royal mall, the windows wide open on a glorious summer morning. I asked Jeremy if he had a job.

"I was grill cook at a diner, but once I started falling apart I had to stop. My fingers went all numb and I'd just stand there by the chopping board with blood flowing over me like strawberry compote."

"Not too good."

"No. And when the numbness went away, I'd get the jitters. Carbon steel blades are no longer a part of my life. A year ago I landed a job doing breakfasts at a tourist-bus hamster wheel of a downtown hotel. Nothing special, but I was able to hold that together, but that's over too as of last month. Out of nowhere, my arms and legs will seize up—not too often, but enough to make kitchens risky. Lately I'm feeling tired a bit more often. Today's a good day for me, but it could all turn to sawdust inside of one breath."

We arrived at the mall a few minutes later, at a chain discount-furniture store called The Rock. We opened its glass doors and I was overwhelmed by hundreds of mattresses and furniture of all types, assembled into no particular departments, the store's air swirling with the fragrance of spooky synthetic molecules. We found an area that seemed to have slightly more mattresses and, not really knowing what to look for, we just stood there looking dumb beneath unflattering yellowy lighting.

"Hi, I'm Ken. Can I help you?" A man approached us—slightly older than me, with a complexion that said, *I like vodka.*

"We need a foldaway bed."

Jeremy said, "And you also need a queen-size bed."

I was baffled. "What?"

"Look, Mom, sorry, but you just can't stay with the twin bed. You're a grown-up woman. Imagine the signal you send out if you bring home some guy and you have a twin bed—like you were fifteen again."

He was right—what *had* I been thinking all these years?

Ken said, "Let's find both. Let's start with the queen-size. Did you have any preference?"

"No." This was all happening so quickly.

"Do you like a hard or soft mattress?"

"I've never thought of that before."

"Let's go try a few."

"Any mattress at all is fine. I really don't need a salesman, and . . ."

"I'm not a salesman, I'm a Sleep Consultant. And before you jump in blindly, let's start you off on this one here." Ken took a sheet of clear solid plastic and spread it out at the foot of the mattress. "Lie down. You can put your feet on the plastic square."

I did, and Ken gave me a thoughtful look. "I see you're a left-handed sleeper."

"A what?"

"A left-handed sleeper. People have handedness in their sleeping too, just as they do in writing or baseball. I sleep on my right side for most of my sleeping."

"What a novel idea."

Ken bent down to look at my back. "Uh-oh."

"What's wrong?"

"Just as I thought: loose spine. You need a mattress with more support. Let's try that one there."

I have to hand it to Ken—he was good. I was bouncing on and off mattresses like the town slut, as Jeremy asked sensible questions. I'd never shopped with someone other than Mother or Leslie before. It was fun, and in the end I found a mattress and box spring combination that had me longing for nightfall.

"Now," said Ken, looking at Jeremy, "let's see what we can find for you. Any specific needs?"

"I'd like one that's quite high up so that it's easy to get on and off."

"A young guy like you?"

"I've got, uh—" Jeremy never liked saying the actual name of the beast.

I said, "MS."

Jeremy added, "Sometimes it's a bit hard to stand up."

It was as if we'd switched on a light bulb within Ken's being. "MS? Why didn't you say so? My brother-in-law has it. Gruesome disease."

I thought this was rude, but Jeremy didn't mind. "Tell me about it!"

Ken said, "What's your name?"

"Jeremy."

"Jeremy, let's find your perfect sleep solution."

We headed toward the folding couches, which had come a long way design-wise since the sixties when I stayed at my grandmother's place.

When it came time to pay for everything, Ken made a tally and asked, "Liz, would you prefer a thirty-dollar discount on the price of your mattress and box spring or a free twenty-inch TV set?"

"Very funny."

"No, I'm serious."

"A free TV?"

He motioned for Jeremy and me to come in closer. "Look, here's the deal. I'm quitting in a few days, so I can tell you. The mattress makers are all locked in a death match right now, and so the deals you can get are insane."

"But a *TV set?*"

"Think about mattresses for a second. They're nothing but air. They're like popcorn at a theatre. They cost about eighteen cents to make. Hell, they're still using the machines they used back in the 1950s. It's all one big scam."

I said that I'd never thought of it like that before.

"Good God, yes. And Jeremy, do you want a gas barbecue to go with your foldaway couch?"

Jeremy said, "Hey, Ken—a gas barbecue would nicely complement my lifestyle."

"Smartass. But you're getting one anyway. What about a job—do you have one?"

"Nope."

"Good. Start here right away, and really play up the MS thing. Do you have a wheelchair?"

"I do."

"Good. It'll up your sales twenty-five percent."

"Really?"

"Oh yeah. The gimp factor. You can't change things, so you might as well work them."

I was appalled but fascinated.

Jeremy asked, "How many people with MS does it take to put in a light bulb?"

Ken didn't know how many.

"Five million—one person to do it, and four million nine hundred and ninety-nine thousand nine hundred and ninety-nine to write depressing on-line web logs."

"You should meet my brother-in-law. He's Mr. Victim. Drives me nuts."

They continued in this vein.

Jeremy asked, "Do I have to fill out an application?"

"I'll get one for you from Shelagh. She's a battleaxe, but tell her you like her sweater and she's in your pocket."

I said, "You can just hire people like that?"

"Absolutely—when the economy is as good as it is now, we have to snare salespeople any way we can. I also get a free microwave for finding a new staffer."

Ken went away to get a form from Shelagh.

"Look, Maw, I done got me a job!"

"Jeremy, isn't it kind of tempting fate to play up your disease?"

"No. Like Ken says, I can't change it, so I may as well work it."

"Are you sure? It's like parking in a handicapped parking stall."

"Not at all."

Jeremy filled out his form, made nice with Shelagh and was slated for sales duty the next day.

* * *

Next stop was Jane's. We drove through downtown to get there. There was an anti-logging protest going on outside the art gallery and we inched along, a car length at a time. We stopped talking for awhile and watched people walking toward the crowd by the gallery's steps. I told Jeremy that if protestors were really smart, and truly wanted to blast out their message, they should protest at night and then set fire to something, *anything*. That'd make the national news, not just the cheesy ultra-local 11:30 p.m. news. He hummed an agreement. I added, "This kind of protesting is so predictable—everybody screaming in front of some old building with nice steps on it and pillars on both sides. All the protestors are really doing is putting a pretty picture frame around their protest."

"Being a bit cynical, Mom?"

"I guess."

We arrived at Jane and Jeremy's apartment building, an East Vancouver 1960s rental unit painted pink and aqua so as to mimic the tropics. Algae, neglect and decades of low-commitment tenants made it seem more like Beirut's shabbier cousin. Dozens of crows clustered in nearby trees, raucously cawing to each other, as they sometimes do.

Just as we were getting out of the car, something small and clattery fell from the sky and exploded on the pavement in front of us. I saw pills strewn all over the sidewalk and road.

"It's Jane." Jeremy looked up and shouted, "What the hell do you think you're doing?"

Jane was on a balcony. "I found your stash, you lying creep."

"That's not my stash. It's prescriptions I've never used."

"I don't believe you."

"You're just mad at me."

"I wonder why!" Suddenly she was holding a boom box above her head. "I am so glad to be getting out of this relationship."

Jeremy shouted, "Don't throw that. It was a present."

Down it came, a blurry high-tech piñata.

"Jane, what is *with* you?"

"I put up with your crap for so, so long, and all that time you were lying."

"I don't lie. I just keep quiet about things."

"I'm sick of your druggie visions, and I'm sick of rescuing you."

"Rescuing me from *what?*"

"From wherever it is you're standing or crawling or lying down. I just want to go to a movie one night and not have to have the ushers carry you out to the car afterwards."

She went inside. Jeremy actually laughed. "She gets like this," he said.

We went inside, where the situation was solely verbal. No more things were tossed.

"Jeremy, I'm just damn *bored* with it all. I can't get mad at you or you'll go into a downspin; I can't be cheerful around you or I look like a phony; I can't try to make you take your pills or I'm Hitler; I can't try to be compassionate with you or else I'm pitying you. I'm sick of trying to be a blank sheet of paper around you. I just want to do normal things like normal people."

Jane went into a room and shut the door. I asked Jeremy why he didn't take his medications.

"If I take too much, I feel like a zombie. I don't feel anything and I don't care about anything. At least with this disease turning my brain into Swiss cheese I get to see great things in my mind. And it's not like the drugs are fixing me. They just mask things."

I looked out the balcony window. Down on the street, I saw crows eating the pills; their crops were bulging full, like Adam's apples.

There was something off-kilter about the apartment. I tried to figure it out while Jeremy fetched a suitcase and began removing things from his drawers and tossing them in. There was an airline tag on the suitcase, from Toronto a few months before. "You went to Toronto?"

"I was in an experimental drug test. It didn't work."

I continued to try to analyze just what made the apartment feel so strange. Jeremy caught me at it. "Everything in the place is geared toward getting up and down easily. Like I told Ken, when I get my brownouts I can't do things like get off a couch easily."

He was right. Clean glasses and plates (all plastic) were piled on the kitchen counter. The couch in front of the TV was elevated so that getting off it wouldn't involve too much lugging up of one's body. The futon was similarly raised. It seemed to me to be borderline geriatric. This saddened me. I saw a wheelchair folded up and my heart sank for him. He saw this.

"Ah, the gimpmobile." He moved it toward the door. "Baby needs new shoes." As he went back into the bedroom, he tapped on Jane's door. "Have you cooled down yet? Come on out."

No reply.

Jeremy could fit all of his clothes into two worn-out suitcases. It struck me that whatever he had in life he'd had to make or find on his own. In my mind I saw him filtering through piles in Salvation Army stores, trying to find items that would help him pass for normal in the world.

Jeremy zipped up the second suitcase and stood outside Jane's door. "Jane?"

Once more, no reply.

"Jane, do you know that futons have been clinically proven to increase wear on your lumbar region by thirty percent?"

No reply.

"As well, a futon's cotton fibres can contain almost two hundred percent more mites than a six-inch-thick foam sheet. A new mattress, shipped directly from the factory, and equipped with a comfortably affordable foam underlay, can make all the difference between insomnia and a good night's sleep."

No reply.

"Also, a new mattress and box spring sprayed with DuPont's Foam-Kote can not only help keep surfaces wipe-clean, but can control mite populations and significantly reduce their nightly harvest of your precious skin cells."

No reply.

"At the moment, purchase of a mattress and box spring combination makes you eligible for an immediate prize reward of a twenty-inch Samsung colour TV, or a George Foreman Indoor-Outdoor Electric Barbecue."

Jane opened the door. "What drug are you on now?"

"No drugs at all. I just got a job."

"You *what?*"

"A job. I'm selling mattresses at Park Royal."

Jane looked at me for confirmation. "It's true."

"Good. Then you can pay me back the two hundred bucks you borrowed to buy those Roman candles from the Indian reservation outside of Seattle last fall."

I said, "Jane, why don't you and I go up on the roof for a cigarette while Jeremy boxes some more of his things."

"Done."

We walked up to the roof, which had a panoramic view of the city: mountains and seagulls and office towers and freighters. It was a children's storybook where readers are asked to spot as many things as they can.

"I must look like such a monster. I'm not a monster."

"Did you hear me saying you were?"

Jane smoked, a surprise, so we lit up.

"I never would have pinned you as being the boom-box-off-the-balcony type, though."

"It felt great."

A seagull landed on the railing not far from us. Once it decided we had no food, it flew off.

"Have you seen him have his visions yet?"

"Yes."

"They give me the creeps."

"I think they're interesting. They're like poems."

"Three days ago, he told me that the sky would go out. Not an eclipse, but rather *pop!*, like a light bulb. Creepy."

"Maybe there was a hidden message there. Maybe at face value they simply register as nonsense, so you have to go deeper."

"No. I just think they're creepy. A week ago he told me he'd had this vision where two ex-lovers passed each other on the street. They'd had an ugly breakup, and their punishment was that each time they saw each other they rusted just a little bit, like robots. In the end they rusted frozen in front of each other. I mean, what the heck is *that?*"

"It's beautiful. Sort of."

"Here's another. He told me that office buildings would collapse, and when they dug through the rubble, the people inside the buildings would be found compressed into diamonds from the force."

"That is beautiful."

She sighed. "Has he conned you into doing any crazy shit yet?"

"Such as?"

"With him, it could be anything—climbing trees to look for coins, digging a huge hole and filling it with balloons—to name two."

"He had me crawling down the highway on my hands and knees in the middle of the day."

"I told you so."

I asked Jane why Jeremy's visions bugged her so much.

"Because I know they're not dreams, so I can't write them off. They really are visions that really *do* come to him."

"So?"

This was obviously important to Jane, and she wanted to express her thoughts correctly. "The thing is, I don't believe in anything. If you don't believe in anything, then where do his visions come from? He makes me doubt my doubt." She stubbed out her cigarette. "He had all that hootenanny religious mumbo-jumbo tossed at him from all his foster families. I thought I could fix him, but no go."

I kept quiet. I may not ever have been in a relationship, but I do know that there's no point trying to fix someone. Instead we discussed the particulars of Jeremy's condition. Jane made it seem like I was adopting a pet. "Heat makes him almost pass out, so no hot baths. I found this vest thing on the Internet that cools him down. If you don't have an air conditioner, buy one. Also, no wheat. It's a killer—bowel issues."

Jeremy was going to be a large undertaking. "Isn't there anybody from one of his families to help him out?"

"You don't want to meet his so-called families. They're all nuts, and all they'll do is hit you up for a loan, and then swipe your purse when you aren't looking."

I couldn't care less. My decision to allow him into my life was like a first kiss.

We lugged Jeremy's stuff downstairs, me carrying the heavy items. In the car I asked Jeremy how he knew all that stuff about mattresses.

"I just made it up as I went."

* * *

At home, I had ten new messages, a personal record, but then they were all from family members.

Jeremy was exhausted. "Let's just watch the news and veg for awhile—maybe make decisions then."

"A perfect idea."

And so we watched the six o'clock news together. It was nice to do something boring with another person. Usually I avoid TV news because sundown is such a hard time, always has been—a time of day that puts italics on your loneliness. Unless I'm in really good shape watching the news at six, I fuzz out into a lonely blur—except when there's a story about a dog trapped in icy waters, whereupon I blubber. If things go from bad to worse, I'll eat a platter of microwaved cinnamon buns at one sitting, and then go for a drive. If I drive when I'm lonely, I easily fall into mind games with other drivers who are lonely too. I've tailgated creeps through an entire rainstorm just to screech at them *Shame on you!* for tossing a cigarette butt out the window near Deep Cove. I don't know what I'm accomplishing by screaming at them. Something is going on inside me; I simply wish I knew what.

Halfway into the news, right after a Burger King commercial, a story appeared about meat production. I'm a carnivore, but, like many people these days, thinking about it too much can give me the willies.

"Why did you make that funny noise?"

"Meat."

"Say no more."

The thing about meat with me, though, is how it speaks to me about the human body. All of us are stuck inside our meaty bodies. I've always imagined that regular people are happy to be inside their bodies, whereas lonely people yearn to ditch their carcasses. I suspect lonely people wish they could forget the whole meat-and-bone issue altogether. We're the people most likely to believe in reincarnation simply because we can't believe we were shackled into our meat in the first place. Lonely people want to be dead, yet we're still not quite ready to go—we don't want to miss the action; we want to see who wins next year's Academy Awards. More to the point, the lonely, like all humans, yearn to meet that somebody who'll make us feel better about being trapped inside our species' meat-and-bone soul containment system. Oh God, I sound like a prison warden.

The phone rang, but Jeremy and I ignored it. It was probably Mother or Leslie.

My family—my condition baffles my family. I doubt Leslie or William can remember a moment in their life when they weren't involved with someone. Mother? She never remarried after my father's car crash. She dates here and there, but she gets waylaid micromanaging her grandkids and bullying her wimpy friends. I don't think she ever gets lonely, but then I never knew about her praying in a closet for Jeremy.

Leslie has a husband, Mike, the breast man, and her kids. I think she has to keep her SUV going at a hundred miles an hour all the time or else she'd be forced to examine her life in solitude, and not be pleased with the results. Look at me: I'm the cliché of a bitter spinster—but who ever really knows what goes on inside a relationship?

"Jeremy, I can't *not* answer the phone for much longer."

"What time is it?"

"Six-thirty."

"Call them back, then, but remember: you hold all the cards, not them."

The next time the phone rang, I picked it up. It was Ken the Sleep Consultant telling Jeremy to be in the next morning at nine-thirty. Almost the moment I hung up, William called.

"Lizzie, it's me, and I just flew back from Europe to meet my new nephew."

"Where are you calling from?"

"A cab. I'm five blocks away. Come down and let me in. Mother says your buzzer's busted."

* * *

William's company is called ImmuDynamics. The name makes his life sound dull, but this isn't the case. William travels the world, bribing government officials and gaining access to databases that tell him where to find a particular country's oldest citizens. If you're under 110, don't even bother wasting William's time. There isn't even a word for people in the age bracket William is interested in. One-hundred-and-tensomethings? No. William says one consistent trait of these creaking old bats is that they almost always want a thousand U.S. dollars, for which they'll cheerfully donate a syringe full of DNA-rich blood.

What does he do with this blood? It's shipped—or perhaps smuggled—back home inside picnic coolers filled with dry ice. The samples are removed and placed into centrifuges or some other wicked machine. From this, ImmuDynamics hopes to locate the data that confers longevity on all those old folk. The thinking is that if they multiply a hoped-for gene into something modular like a slice of processed cheese or baloney, they can then slip it into whatever parts of a sick person's DNA sandwich need beefing up. William says every family has at least two trap doors: weak hearts, cancer-prone breasts or prostates, lazy livers or Alzheimer's or what have you. Fix those trap doors and life goes on and on and on. Frankly, I don't see the point, life being nasty, brutish and dull as it already is; but then I'm not the eighty-six-year-old founder of a Fortune 500 company with a gouty toe and kidney cancer.

* * *

"William is going to be here in a minute."

"Back from Europe?"

"Yup. How are you feeling?"

"Bet you fifty bucks I can sell him a mattress."

"William? Good luck. You're on."

Walking down the stairs, I felt like Jeremy and I had morphed into a pair of circus carnies. My brother was knocking at the door. "William, you look like hell."

"So do you. I came right back as soon as I heard the news."

"You didn't have to."

"Lizzie, let me enjoy this."

Once I was inside, I made quick introductions, and Jeremy shook William's hand from the couch. William squinted his eyes in a way that said, *What a rude little shit, he can't even stand up to meet me.*

"Jeremy has MS, William."

"Right! What awful luck. Lizzie, got any booze?"

"I have ouzo. I've no idea what it tastes like. It's been here since the Reagan administration."

"I'll chance it." William turned to look at Jeremy. "So, it's really true, then. You're you."

"Yes, I'm me."

"Let's have a good look at you, then."

"William, he's not a cocker spaniel—"

Jeremy said, "No, it's okay." He sat up straight.

William, being male, looked only for bits of himself in Jeremy's face. I walked in with the ouzo and a glass, and he said, "He looks a bit like me, don't you think?"

"Oh, brother. You, you, you."

"My ouzo. Well, it's better than nothing." He turned to Jeremy and lifted his glass in a toast. "Great to meet you. Ghastly news about the MS." He drank a shot and said, "Bugger me, that's dreadful stuff. Pour another, please."

Jeremy, almost as a joke, asked William what the movie was on the plane.

"Something with zombies and car crashes. At the end of it, melon-breasted cheerleaders save the planet."

Jeremy said, "I feel like a zombie a lot of the time."

"Well, you would."

"The only thing that makes it better is a good night's sleep."

"I'm not surprised."

"Yes, a good night's sleep is crucial."

Sly of Jeremy to cut to the sales chase so ruthlessly. I caused a brief detour by asking, "What's the deal with zombies—does anybody know?"

"What do you mean?"

"Zombies are like normal people until they're bitten by another zombie. Once they're bitten, why don't they just die? Why do they have to become zombies too?"

Jeremy said, "When you become a zombie, your soul vanishes. There's no heaven or hell for you—there's absolutely nothing—which is why zombies are so terrifying. Your relationship to the profound is taken away from you, and there's no hope of retrieving it."

William swirled his second ouzo's dregs in the glass. "Well that's fucking cheerful."

Jeremy said, "Growing up, my parents used zombies as metaphors for people trapped in secular humanism."

I said, "Some of Jeremy's foster families were religious."

"Families?" William changed the subject. "Where's Mother? Where's Leslie?"

"I haven't responded to their messages yet."

"Smart decision. Jeremy, have some ouzo. You too, Lizzie."

I found myself fetching two more glasses. William poured ouzo into them and said, "Cheers, then—welcome to the family."

We clinked and drank the Greek turpentine. William yawned.

Jeremy said, "Tired?"

"Jet lag. First class was full and—*oof!*—those torture chamber airline seats in coach."

"Bad back support can wreck not only your sleep but your waking time as well."

"Oof. Tell me about it."

"How many hours a night do you normally sleep?"

"Me? Six. Maybe six and a half if I'm lucky."

"You could fix that so easily. And without chemicals, too."

"Really?"

"Oh yeah."

Within a half-hour William was snoring on my bed, Jeremy had sold a king suite and I was fifty dollars poorer. My annoying sister-in-law, Nancy, was coming to pick up William, who was groggy from being ripped out of a deep alpha-wave sleep, and cursing the ouzo. "You could strip paint with that stuff."

"Go wash up. You know Nancy likes to nitpick your appearance."

In the living room, Jeremy said, "I'm going to paint one of your walls for you."

"What makes you want to do that?"

"I don't understand people who can only paint a room if all the walls are the same colour—or people who move into a house, stick the sofa here, a table there and a picture on a wall, and then say to themselves, *Finished. I'll never have to think about this room ever again.* A house is just as alive as the person who lives in it."

"Which wall? What colour?"

"By the phone. Red. Japanese lacquer red."

The notion of a red lacquer wall was, at that point in my life, only on the cusp of imaginability. "Really?"

"It'll take five coats, but it'll make this place live and breathe."

"Painting walls is hard work."

"*Pffff!* Painting walls is nothing. It was another one of those things I did when I moved into a new foster home to make me seem useful."

I heard stones tapping at my window. It was Nancy. I went down to let her in. In the elevator she was too busy scolding Hunter and Chase to ask about Jeremy. Inside the apartment, William looked awful. Nancy said, "Comb your hair." Then I introduced her to Jeremy, but she was restrained in her greeting.

Chase said, "Mom told us you had a disease. It's that telethon disease where they put you in a wheelchair and then people push you down a hill and you die."

William and his family got into a squabble and I wanted a few moments to myself. I slipped into my bedroom, shut and locked the door, then sat on my bed—nice and cool and cottony. I lay down and felt the sheets draining the heat from my body. I was intensely happy to have this room to myself, and to not be out there with the family.

William knocked on my door. "Lizzie? Lizzie, drag your ass out here. I need you to help civilize things."

I said nothing.

"Have it your way, then."

I heard Nancy ask, "What's *her* problem?"

"Just having one of her mood swings."

What? I ran and opened the door, ignoring William. "Nancy, I am *not* having a mood swing. I've only ever had one mood in my entire life, and you *know* that. It's impossible for me to have moods between which I can swing. Just be quiet for once, okay?"

William said, "Time to go. I'll call tomorrow."

Goodbyes were made, and before the sky was fully dark, Jeremy and I were both asleep.

* * *

The summer of 1997, Hale-Bopp rode the sky above Hollyburn Mountain every night for weeks on end. Sometimes it was buttery and weak, and sometimes it looked like felt cut with blunt kindergarten scissors—but not once did I ever get used to seeing the damn thing up there. It wasn't natural. Nothing in the sky seems natural to me except the sun and the stars. Even the moon, for lack of a better word, is on probation. Why the thing can't just stay full all the time drives me nuts. Crescent? Waxing? Waning? Oh, just make up your mind.

I'm grinding my gears.

Okay . . .

I suppose it's important here to reinforce yet again that I'm overweight, nay, fat. I think all of us have a set of generic characteristics in our heads that we employ when we read stories. I've always been perplexed by books in which too much emphasis is placed on describing the protagonist—"Her hair was the colour of milk and almonds, and she walked with a pronounced limp," or, "He was wiry and taut. His red hair formed a halo." You catch my drift. In the end, what I call our "universal protagonists" fill the bills. It doesn't matter what the book is about, or when or where it's set, out come our inner heroes, as bland and predictable as any TV station's six o'clock news team. My suspicion is that the universal female protagonist looks like a soccer mom in a lamé gown, while the man could be a roofing contractor dressed for cocktails. I, of course, am neither. I think the truth is important here, if only as a technicality. Let me describe myself a little . . .

I'm overweight, and my clothes are . . . *serviceable*—usually loose fabrics because they conceal my roundness. Bras? Don't get me going. I like rattan purses because I can carry more things around with me that way—usually books, which I read alone in a booth at White Spot, where I also note the way people react to my presence. The little teenage girls in their spray-on denim and sparkling lip gloss take one look at me, recognize me as a cosmic danger signal, then never look at me again. Men of all ages don't notice me, period. To them, I'm a fern. Women older than, say, thirty notice me and treat me kindly, but once they think I'm not looking, their faces betray depressed interiors—I'm what will happen to them if they don't play their cards right. Restaurant staff, I suspect, are always waiting for me to be difficult, sending the hamburger back because the patty is overcooked or expressing dissent because the white wine is too vinegary. Why? Maybe they think I'm so desperate for interaction that a squabble is better than nothing.

I sometimes imagine spending a hundred grand on cosmetic surgery—making myself bionic, or a clone of Leslie—but I never will. One simple reason is that patients have to be picked up by a family member; taxis aren't allowed—not even limos. The thought of Mother castigating me in the car while I'm swaddled in sterile linen mummy wrapping scotches *that* idea—wisdom teeth were bad enough. While I like Leslie—my glamorous sister the milk robot with her *Hindenburg* bosom—our closeness is based on her being the pretty one and me being the invisible one. She'd invent a reason why she couldn't drive me. William probably would, but . . . I just don't want to have anything done. I just don't. I can't put words to it. It's primal.

So don't imagine me as your universal protagonist. I am not Jaclyn Smith or Christy Turlington. I'm not Demi Moore, and I'm not whoever is the Demi Moore equivalent of your era. I'm me. I'm real.

* * *

I felt awkward driving Jeremy to work with his folding wheelchair, but he was cavalier. "And in any event, I might need it for real."

"Aren't you tempting fate somewhat?"

"Nope. And besides, I'm taking my meds again now, so I won't be locking up or passing out."

"Not seeing any visions, either?"

"Probably not."

"You know best."

I walked alongside him into The Rock, into its eerily timeless aura of chemicals, bleak furniture and unflattering lighting. I said goodbye and watched him wheel up to the counter. For the first time I witnessed the impact he and the gimpmobile made on strangers. Behind his back the women were enacting *Isn't-he-tragically-adorable?* swoons, hands clasped over their hearts. Shoppers saw him coming a mile away and parted for him reverentially. It reminded me of high school when a football player walked into class, and all the girls went silent and twirled their hair.

Of course Jeremy was totally aware of his effect, and the little ham played it up for all he could. I thought, *Good for him,* but his shamelessness still worried me. Driving away from the mall and over the bridge to work that morning, I felt like I was entering a new life but was somehow being dragged back into an old one. Life before Jeremy seemed so far in the past. Usually on the way to work I'd be obsessively making lists and planning the evening to come, doing what I could to minimize loneliness. Instead I was wondering if Jeremy was still going to see his visions now that he'd started taking his meds again. I thought of what a shame it would be for him to lose them. They were bizarre, but they were genuinely his and his alone.

I then began to wonder how I'd feel if I'd had a girl instead of Jeremy. I'd be equally as protective, and equally as blessed, yet I'd feel awkward about looking her in the eyes. Why? Look at the eyes of a single woman at twenty, at thirty and at forty. I'm thinking of Jane, say. At twenty, she can't wait to be corrupted—is even giddy at the prospect of so much inner fuel just waiting to be burned: *Use me! Dump me! Turn me on to freaky stuff! Amyl nitrate! Whips! Just pick me!* But at thirty, those same eyes will send a different message: *Okay, I know what it's like to get burned, and just don't try to burn me, okay? I can see the tan line left by the wedding ring, and *69 tells me you live in a suburb with lots of trees and plenty of elementary schools and soccer fields.* Obviously, there's a bit of fuel remaining—just enough to get you back to civilization, should things go horribly wrong.

But look at those eyes at forty. There's a potent echo from two decades before: *Use me! Dump me! Turn me on to freaky stuff! Pick me!* But at the same time, the fuel's pretty much spent, and you don't want to be used and dumped and exposed to leather and enemas, and any guy you meet is going to look at your papers, see the absence of long relationships or marriage, and quietly move on. Maybe he's the one who's damaged goods, but does it matter? Sixty seconds after he's dropped you off for the last time, he's singing along to Supertramp on the AM radio. You're not even a memory; you're a speed bump. Were you asking for much? *Just don't interrupt my daily routines, and please enjoy watching* Law & Order *reruns as much as I do.*

I don't know if I'd want to see any of this in the eyes of a daughter of mine, regardless of age. The change would be too hard to bear.

* * *

My return to the office was a non-event. I felt like some sort of magic rock that creates no ripple when thrown in water. Donna gophered her head over her cubicle wall and asked me how my jaws felt, and the word "Fine" was barely out of my mouth before her head bobbed down and she was on the phone with some guy selling motherboards.

I booted up and looked at my screen. My usual ritual when beginning my day had always been to count the number of days until I die based on government statistics telling me that women born in 1960 could expect to live to seventy-six. In my mind, my birthday in 2036 has been my checkout date. This sounds macabre, but how many of us quietly do this—treat our lives like time-coded dairy products on the fridge's middle shelf, silently fermenting beside a doomed bag of lettuce? Now, for the first time in years, I didn't feel like checking my expiry date.

I also have another program that tells me my one thousandth birthday will fall on a Friday. My five hundredth birthday will fall on Monday. I used to have fun seeing whether or not my one millionth birthday fell on a statutory holiday. But that morning when I returned to work? I checked my birthday in a billion years, and it falls on a Wednesday, and the whole death obsession seemed a bit passé. Thinking about my death like this was, I suppose, akin to my fascination with actors portraying corpses onscreen.

Theodore and Mike from the LAN team came by to ask me if I wanted to join their lottery pool. I thought about this for a moment and passed.

"You sure, Liz? 'Embittered Co-worker Goes on Lottery-Loss Bloodbath Murder Spree.'"

"I've had enough fate for one week."

They looked at me blankly.

"I'll pass."

"Your loss." And they were gone.

Lonely lives are filled with ritual to ward off the void of evenings spent alone, but for the first time in my life I didn't feel this way. It took me an hour at my keyboard, doing nothing, for this to sink in. I spaced out and lost all sense of time. When I snapped out of this, I thought of all the times in my life when I'd been driving from A to B and suddenly realized I'd gone five miles with no memory of having driven them. And with that came the feeling that I got away with something. That sort of sums up my pre-Jeremy existence: arranging my life so that I could forget about it while it was happening.

The Dwarf To Whom I Report came to visit, me still staring at the computer's empty window.

"Hello in there—"

I looked up at him. "Oh—hi, Liam."

"Hello, Liz. Are you feeling better?"

"Pretty much."

"How are your teeth?"

"My teeth?" I was briefly stumped. "Oh, dear—my surgery—yes, I'd forgotten it. My teeth are fine. Couldn't be better."

"And your week away?"

"It's hard to tell where to begin, Liam." *Hale-Bopp? The emergency ward?* "It's been very full, really."

In a conspiratorial tone he said, "Donna said you were looking swollen and bruised."

"She would, then, wouldn't she?"

Liam laughed. "Yes. She would."

Liam . . .

Liam is short, or, rather, he's shorter than me, and I'm short. (And yes, I'm fat and have red wavy hair.) He is a fussy man, as if he had read and taken to heart grooming advice from previous eras—old mildewed *Esquire*s with articles on extinct subjects such as Richard Nixon or key parties. But I had only to look at his shoes and any aura vaporized. His shoes spoke to me, and what they said was, "$69.95." They were made from the dull pigskin leather specific to medicine balls and dog collars. He had five discrete looks, one for every working day—and all of them subverted by shoes he probably traded at a flea market for a car battery with the cables thrown in. No. He bought them at the Metrotown mall on sale for $49.95 and thinks they're functional. It's just so—*Liam.* A failure of judgment at the final, most critical step.

Liam also wears a *Raiders of the Lost Ark*–style fedora. A few years back he affected a three-day-stubble look that had the girls in Data yucking it up for weeks on end.

But wait a second—wasn't I saying earlier that physical descriptions of people are pointless? Well, yes—when it comes to the hero and heroine. I suppose that for incidental characters, description is a possibility. I've always felt sorry for those actors in movies and on TV whom you recognize instantly but whose name you'll never know. They're simply familiar, and that is the essence of their employability.

When Liam went away, I opened some files and poked at them as if they were liver and onions, and was glad when the phone rang. It was Jeremy, who'd just made his first sale. I said, "Congratulations, you little huckster."

"It's Ken's last day and I wanted to impress him. It was so easy. It was this woman who had yuppie flu, or twentieth-century disease or whatever they're calling it now. We both lay down on the Supreme Ultra-rest combo—Ken's right, by the way, it's all a total scam—and then it was so funny, we both fell asleep, and Ken came and woke us up after nearly an hour, and bingo, the sale was mine. And she slipped me her phone number."

"Congratulations again. How old was she?"

"Eighty-six or something."

"No, how old was she really?"

"Okay. Fortyish."

"A good forty or a scary forty?"

"Good. But I got the feeling her standards are too high, so no matter how hard she tries, she always falls for the same guy."

"I had the yuppie flu once, you know."

"BS."

"No, really. Ten years ago—for almost a year. Mother told me it was all in my head and wouldn't listen if it came up. Leslie said that I should try having a kid and *then* come to her to discuss having no energy. William said I wasn't a yuppie and that the yuppie flu is horse crap anyway."

"But it's not."

"No. But I only believed it because I knew I'd had it. Otherwise I'd think it was crap too."

"How'd you manage?"

"After every test in the book came back negative, I resigned myself to it."

"*It?* Describe *it.*"

"Waking up, feeling good for maybe ten minutes, and then feeling like a dying houseplant for the rest of the day. No energy. No nothing. I blamed everything—dairy, yeast, mineral deficiencies, lack of sunlight, too much sunlight, alcohol, Epstein-Barr."

"What happened?"

"It just stopped one day. No reason. It just stopped."

I could tell we were getting too close to discussing MS on the level Jeremy hated, the meat-and-potatoes symptom level, as opposed to Ken the Sleep Consultant's ink-black humour. He changed the subject. "You know, there's a lot to be said for having a small, manageable dream. I'm going to set the sales record for this branch. Just you watch."

"I have no doubt."

"Gotta go. Let's discuss dinner later today." He hung up.

It's a measure of my social naïveté that when Donna gophered her head up again and asked, "Who was that?"

I didn't tell her to screw off. Instead, I said, "That was my son."

Well, her eyes bungeed out of her skull, but she quickly roped them in. "Really?"

"Yes."

"What's his name?"

"Jeremy."

"What grade is he in?"

"No grade. He's twenty."

I could imagine Donna's brain at work: *Is he Liz's biological child or is he something else? Why has Liz been so secretive about him until now? Twenty? Maybe he's hot. Maybe he's . . .* It was fun watching her be tortured by curiosity.

I said, "I have to finish these files right now, Donna. Let's talk later."

"What are you doing for lunch?"

"Oh, I have plans already." I didn't, but this only made her torture worse. Quite cheerfully I opened up my files and went to work, not giving a rat's ass about what they contained. Jeremy was this new paint that had rendered me visible to the world.

* * *

At home after work, Jeremy and I swapped stories about our days as we ate some pasta with artichoke hearts. He'd whipped it up from scratch, and I think it was one of the happiest meals of my life. Even the smallest of life's daily details—new toner cartridge for the copier, a faulty traffic light on Marine Drive—seemed charmed and profound.

Jeremy told me about a guy who came into the store only for a nap. It was engrossing.

After this, we watched a *Law & Order* rerun on TV, heckling the program with the love and crabbiness that comes from addiction to a specific show. Mother came over shortly after nine to drop off some old clothes of William's she thought Jeremy might like—Mother always needs a pretext for a visit. Before I knew it, I was in bed and falling asleep, content to repeat this day for a thousand years if I could.

The week melted by. It was inconsequential, yet glorious. The weather was warm, and we ate on restaurant patios.

At work, out of my newly discovered motherly concern, I phoned Social Services, to fill in some of the gaps in Jeremy's history. It was a gamble, as they legally didn't have to tell me anything, and I certainly wasn't about to tell Jeremy any of this. I thought that if I didn't call I'd feel like the sort of mother who leaves the kids playing with thumbtacks while going out to find a fix. I made a lunch appointment on Thursday to meet with Kayla, someone who actually knew Jeremy from way back, and who would bring along what knowledge she could.

We met at a Japanese place two blocks from the office. Kayla was an efficient redhead with one of those faces that looks the same at ten or forty or eighty. We sat down and wiped our hands with hot *oshibori* towels.

"From what I can gather, Jeremy was hard to place with families. He tended to get into trouble more often than not—"

"What sort of trouble?"

"There seems to have been a consistent problem of things going missing—"

"What kinds of things?"

"Not money, but small items, enough to spook the foster parents."

I filed this away with the stories of the stolen mozzarella and the family photos. I asked Kayla if Jeremy sold items to support a drug problem, but she didn't think Jeremy was into drugs.

"That issue never came up."

It was a difficult lunch, because Kayla was restricted in what she could tell me and there were blocks of silence.

"What about his MS—how come you people couldn't have helped him more?"

"He was diagnosed at seventeen, but after eighteen there's nothing we can do. He's an adult."

"His families didn't care?"

"To be honest, no. Not much."

"And the disease can accelerate that quickly?"

"Yup."

I wanted to grab the whole wretched foster system, Kayla included, and smush it into a ball, then step on the ball and crush it. I was furious, but there was no point in letting it show. Kayla was already pushing the rules on my behalf. It was an unsatisfactory meal by any standards, and we both knew it.

Kayla tried making a call on her cellphone, but the battery was dead, so she came up to the office to use a Landover phone. I was in the kitchen getting a coffee when I heard Jeremy walk in. He was speaking to Donna, who was at the fax machine. I looked out. "Jeremy?"

"Hi, Mom. I had the afternoon off, so I thought I'd come visit."

"That's wonderful. How'd you get here?"

"Cabbed."

Donna was dazed and tripping over her words. It was interesting watching her turn into a mumbling cheerleader. Jeremy was pulling out all the stops, using what he called his "winning smile"—a rehearsed showman's grin that instantly swung a room his way. No wonder he sold so many mattresses. The three of us made small talk. This tiny discussion defined my life's BEFORE photo and its AFTER version. I've never felt so popular, before or since.

It was as the three of us were discussing box springs that Kayla came down the hall from where she'd been phoning. Jeremy turned around, saw her and collapsed on the spot.

* * *

What I haven't mentioned here are Jeremy's notes. I found them on scraps of paper around the condo, notes marred by coffee rings, phone numbers and ketchup stains. He obviously had no intention to keep or archive them; he simply blurted them onto paper and forgot them. But I saved them. I brought them to work with me, and kept them in my upper drawer along with Post-it notes, decongestant tablets, Sharpie pens and skin-tone concealer.

Jeremy's handwriting was appalling—a scrawl, really, not that mine's much better. Penmanship has gone the way of typewriters and vinyl records.

Here follow some of the ones I have here now, their spelling corrected . . .

guns shooting at loaves of bread

—

coyotes stumbling down an empty freeway. eyes are milky

—

There's too much sun.
The sun shines whenever and wherever it likes. Night is old fashioned.

—

WHERE is the correct path?

—

if time had to begin then it has to end at some point, too.

what if God exists but he doesn't really like people very much?

We never discussed these notes. I'm not even sure if Jeremy knew I kept them, or if he thought I'd tossed them away. After he began working and taking his medication, his visions vanished, and I wanted these paper scraps as proof that there still existed this other Jeremy inside of him who pondered such things. I mean, if he gave me the word, I'd have been right back there on the highway again, crawling toward the west.

Life is hard. We all need something to believe in, even if it's cockamamie. I'd never thought much about belief one way or the other until Jeremy entered my life. His visions marked the first signs of an awakening within myself. Poor Jeremy had spent his childhood being bandied from family to family like a porn novel in a summer camp. It was hard for him to put his faith in any idea larger than his immediate world. We'd ended up marooned on the same beach. Curiously, one definition of health is that you have the same disease as all of your neighbours; in this sense, he and I were the picture of health.

Was I falling in love with my son? It must sound like it, but no. However, I *was* realizing that I loved him very much indeed.

* * *

When Jeremy collapsed, he hit his head on a planter that held a ficus tree. There was no blood, and he was only out for about thirty seconds, but I thought I should take him to Emergency.

He didn't like the fuss we made about him in the office, and in the car he was silent, angry at me for speaking with Kayla. I said, "I can see your point. It might seem like I was going behind your back, but I was only doing what any mother would do."

"What did she tell you?"

"Almost nothing. Is there something I should know?"

We were on Marine Drive headed east. The car was dirty, and light catching the dirt made it hard to see what lay ahead.

"Pull over."

I did. I turned off the engine. I asked him, "What's up?"

"When I was thirteen, there was this one family I was with for maybe three months. They were great. Sunday was like Thursday with them. They didn't believe in anything but cars and skiing and schnauzer dogs. We went to restaurants all the time and they gave me ten bucks a week as allowance, with no lectures or anything."

"Why'd you leave?"

"I woke up one night and I was in between them on their bed. I went mental, and ran down to the RCMP detachment office in my underwear. It was December and I froze, but they didn't drive me back to the house. I have a hunch I wasn't the first kid to run away."

"Okay."

"I can tell you more."

"Okay."

It has been said, by someone far wiser than myself, that nobody is boring who is willing to tell the truth about himself. To narrow this down further, someone equally wise said that the things that make us ashamed are also the things that make us interesting. And so Jeremy continued, mimicking some long-gone foster parent, "*What's faith unless you constantly expose it to challenges? What are your own ideas if they can be so easily eaten by the ideas of others?*

"If I've come away with anything, it's that the moment foster parents start asking about your soul, you're toast. The moment you start challenging their ideas, you're gone. They'll always talk about surrender, but it's never really to God—they want you to surrender to *them.* Most of those foster people?—they're just scamming some soiled nickels from the government."

"It can't be that bad. I mean—" It was thoughtless of me to interrupt, but if he minded, he didn't show it.

"When you're tired is when you're at your weakest. When you're tired is when they strike. Not tired in your soul, but just tired from a day of chopping wood or chainsawing blackberry thickets, and maybe after you've drunk half a mickey of rye and tried to forget the family that came before the one you're with now. It's after dinnertime, and there's nothing on TV, so you're up in your room wishing there was a song able to describe your life on the radio, and you're cursing the aurora borealis for interfering with radio waves from real places like Spokane or Vancouver or Seattle. And then suddenly there's a knock on the door—assuming they're that polite, or maybe crafty enough to use politeness as a tactic. So you open the door and in they walk, maybe angry, or maybe filled with fake concern, but somehow they manage to end up on your bed, and somehow, no matter how you position your body, they end up being too close to you. *I'm your custodian—trust me—and if you don't trust me, just go with it, because choice isn't an option for you, is it? I've seen your record.* So you fight for yourself as much as you can for your age and size."

"Jeremy, I don't know how much more of this I ought to be hearing."

"You're the one who called Kayla."

"That's not fair. I wanted to find out more about your MS."

"I'm so tired of people seeing me as a walking disease."

"I don't see you that way."

Each car that passed made my Honda jiggle. I didn't know what to say, and then suddenly I did. "You're mad at me for putting you up for adoption in the first place."

Silence.

"Jeremy, I was sixteen."

Silence.

"If I could redo it, I would. I don't know what else to say."

We drove past a bunch of teenagers holding a car wash for breast cancer research. They seemed to me to be younger than children, Oompah-loompahs. Muppets. Imps.

That's where we left it, unspoken, knowing in our hearts that exploring the issue much further would yield no bonuses, that to go further would be to go only downhill—at least for the time being.

We drove on to the hospital, Jeremy with his hand out the window, making it swoop up and down in the breeze.

* * *

An X-ray revealed no damage, and we were both relieved simply to go home and graze the cupboards for dinner. As an added bonus, we discovered an episode of *Law & Order* that neither of us had seen, and were well engrossed in it when there was a knock on the door. We made a face at each other, meaning, *Should we open it?* I decided I'd better, and when I did, I found Liam in the hallway.

"Hi, Liz. Can I come in?"

"Uh, sure."

We walked into the living room. "Jeremy, this is The Dw—*Liam,* my boss."

Liam sat down. "What's the show you're watching?"

"*Law & Order.*"

"Never seen it."

"It's newish."

The thing about a favourite show is that it has the capacity to obliterate all real-world action short of nuclear war. Liam knew Jeremy and I were emotionally unavailable until it ended. When it did, Liam said, "Liz, I hear Jeremy had a bit of a fall today."

Jeremy cut in, "I'm fine."

"We went to Emergency, and X-rays showed no damage."

"That's good."

Jeremy was mischievous and turned to Liam and said, "So, are you two an item?"

"No. I just came to see if you were okay."

"I said I was fine."

"He's fine, Liam."

"That's good, then."

Liam didn't make any gesture to leave, and as I'd never had guests before, I didn't have any idea how to get them to leave. "Would you like a coffee?"

"Please. That'd be nice."

I went to make it in the kitchen. A spate of pointed silence finally forced Liam's hand. "I'm just coming back from choir practice."

"Hmm. Really?"

Jeremy said, "Mom's a really good singer."

Liam looked at me. "Really now?"

My stomach did the *let's karaoke!* lunge. "Jeremy, I can't sing."

"Yes you can. I know you can, because I'm a good singer, and genetically you need two good singers to make a kid who can also sing." He turned to Liam. "It's a fact. Mom hides her light under a bushel."

Singing scares me. I only ever do it in the car, otherwise someone might hear me. Someone might know how I'm feeling inside. I'll somehow bungle it. I'd spent a lifetime concealing my ability, even to the point of standing mute during "Happy Birthdays" over the years.

Liam said, "Liz—sing something for us."

"The neighbours might hear."

"Mom, do you even know who your neighbours are?"

I didn't—I still don't. Mine is not that kind of building. "It doesn't matter. I still don't want them to hear me."

Liam said, "Sing the solo version of the Flower Duet."

"Liam, that song is done to death. British Airways has wrecked it for me."

"Mom, if you sing, I'll sing something too. But you have to sing first."

How could I resist hearing my own son sing? "Oh God, very well." I realized I hadn't sung in ages. Singing voices vanish as quickly as a bodybuilder's triceps in the absence of training. I walked to the sink, poured a quick glass of water and contemplated the song to come, "Viens, Malika," from Delibes's *Lakmé*. It's a good song, a classical staple that is to the highbrow world what the Carpenters' "We've Only Just Begun" is to AM radio.

I came back into the room. "Remember, you two requested this." I spent the next minute pumping out the song's most signature portion, sad and lovely. I rather surprised myself. The two men clapped. I sat down and motioned Jeremy to stand.

He didn't need a glass of water. He readied himself, and then frightening almost-but-not-quite-musical sounds came from his lungs. Buzz saws? Bees? I thought it was a seizure of some kind, and was halfway off my seat before he motioned me to sit. He went on for maybe half a minute.

There was a pause. I asked, "Jeremy, what was that?"

"That was your song sung backwards."

I said, "You're kidding."

"No, not kidding at all. Want another?"

"How did you ever learn to do that?"

"I never would have known I could do it except that, when I was eleven, one of my foster brothers and I would play records backwards to look for satanic messages. The adults thought it was very devout of us."

"Liz, can you sing backwards too?" Liam asked.

"No."

Liam asked me if I had a tape recorder. I had one left over from the 1980s, and I went to fish it out of the cupboard. I'd liked it because it was so easy to stop and start. I used it for voice practice in the old days, when I was a bit braver about singing.

I came back in. "I can rig it to play backwards if I fiddle with these two switches for a second." I prepared the machine.

"What song do you want me to do?" Jeremy asked.

Liam, AM to the core, said, "Try this." He sang "The Wreck of the *Edmund Fitzgerald*," emoting with his hands an Italian *mio cuore*. It was painful.

Jeremy said, "Cakewalk."

I turned on the player, and Jeremy held it to his mouth and made his disturbing air-being-sucked-in noises for a minute. He stopped and I hit rewind. It was the song, not exactly perfect, but certainly better than most people can sing.

"Well, what do you know?"

Liam asked, "How rare is that—being able to sing backwards?"

"It's pretty freakish. It has a name. It's called *melodioanagramaticism*. It's a brain-wiring quirk, like Tourette's. I can only do about thirty seconds at a go."

"You didn't know your son could sing backwards?"

"Long story."

"Why don't the pair of you come visit my choir? It can't hurt, and everyone will get a charge out of your reverse singing."

"I don't know . . ." I'd never been invited to do something like this before; I had no idea of how to handle such a situation.

Liam's request took me back in time to about five years before. I'd been downtown buying pastries. I was in my heels and good dress, feeling metropolitan and go-gettery, a soft harbour breeze on my face, when I walked one-foot, two-foot into eight-inch-deep wet concrete. I looked down and my feet were gone. I tried lifting them, but they were held in tightly. People walking by were unsure if it was a prank, and kept on walking. I then removed my feet, shoes trapped in the concrete (still there, too, I imagine), and walked with dignity to my car, parked four storeys up in an open-air parkade. I drove home in my encrusted pantyhose as if it had never occurred.

Jeremy answered Liam's invitation on my behalf. "She'd love to."

"Great, then. We meet over near Deep Cove. Liz, I'll give you details tomorrow."

I wanted to end the day as quickly as possible, to be lost in a lovely general anaesthetic dreamless sleep—what I hope death will be like.

Liam stood up but put his hand to the small of his back.

Jeremy said, "Back troubles?"

"The joys of getting older."

"Almost all back trouble can be fixed with the right mattress. What sort of sleep system do you have at home?"

"Sleep system?"

Damn him. Within ten minutes he'd made another sale. I was in my housecoat. I looked into the living room, said good night and went to visit dreamland.

* * *

The next day at work was Casual Friday, a repugnant custom that permits the men to dress like teenage boys and the girls like tramps. After years of badgering, my co-workers still didn't grasp the fact that I was never going to crumble on this issue. Donna was the worst, but she didn't show up that morning, and I counted my blessings in being spared the no-team-spirit lecture.

Around ten-thirty my phone rang. Jeremy. "You'll never guess what I just won."

"What?"

"A George Foreman mean and lean fat-reducing grill machine."

"Huh?"

"A barbecue."

"Oh. That's wonderful—now we have two. How did you win it?"

"I did double my monthly sales quota in one week."

"Congratulations."

"Again I have to say it, Mom, there's a lot to be said for having a small and manageable dream."

"That's a very good philosophy."

"If I make one more sale by five o'clock, I get a seven hundred–watt microwave oven too."

Jeremy sounded happy, and this made me happy too. "You're a marvel, you are."

"You'll never guess who just bought the mattress that sent me into barbecue territory."

"Who?"

"Donna."

"*What?*"

"Donna from your office. She bought a ten-inch-thick queen with a deluxe quilted cover atop a four-inch top layer of breathable, open-cell temperature-sensitive viscoelastic foam, *plus* a single layer of a patented airflow system."

"Oh."

"It gets better. The model comes with a certificate proving that non-toxic materials have been used in its manufacture. It also promises a firm orthopaedic support and keeps its shape for many years."

"You don't say."

"Absolutely. And the mattress body is pelted with a soft, naturally treated terry/velour—seventy-five percent cotton and twenty-five percent polyester. It's the latest in anti-mite and anti-allergy technology, with zippers on all four sides for easy removal."

"That Donna is one lucky customer."

"She got a free barbecue, too."

"I'm speechless."

"We're going on a date on Sunday."

I didn't know what to say.

"Mom?"

"A date?"

"Yeah. Bowling. I've never done it, and I want to do it while I still can."

"Jeremy, the woman is ten years older than you."

"So?"

I bit my lip. "It'll be fun for you."

"I hope so. Wait a second—Mom—there's a non-senior citizen staring at mattresses by the entrance. I have to bag this one."

"Catch that brass ring."

"Thanks. Let's order pizza for dinner."

"Roger."

If nothing else, Jane was certainly out of the picture.

Donna didn't show up at all that day, perhaps too embarrassed to look me in the eye, cradle-snatcher that she was. It was better that she didn't. Her absence gave me time to assess the situation and decide what I was going to do. I'd barely had him to myself a week and suddenly I had to *share* my son? No!

But . . .

But . . .

I figured that I might not like Donna, but she wasn't evil. She was probably even a lonely soul in the making, a future Liz, in spite of her thin figure and straight, unwilful hair. On the surface, Donna had all the social bonuses I lacked, and yet the world had changed so much for these younger girls that it was getting easier and easier to become a Liz Dunn.

I also had to keep in mind that Jeremy came with an expiration date on him. His life would be shorter than I could hope for myself. I wasn't about to mess with what time remained solely because of selfishness. So I decided to try to be big about Donna.

This strategy came to me during lunch, which I ate by myself in my Honda down near the Saskatchewan Wheat Pool silos, where a thousand pigeons snacked on spilled grains from CN railway cars. How many times had I eaten there, looking at the pigeons, so easily fed and satisfied? Hundreds. That afternoon I decided I couldn't eat there any more, and nor have I eaten there since.

Back at the office, I tried to catch up on my work backlog, yet I felt like I was only wasting time. Nothing about my job felt pressing or valuable, save for the fact that Liam became crabby if it wasn't done quickly enough. The Dwarf himself hadn't yet sent me details of the upcoming choir practice, and I was hoping he'd forgotten it, but Liam's not the type to forget that kind of thing, so I adopted a "take whatever comes" attitude.

At my desk, my rate of errors went up, and the little *blink-blink* noise my monitor made began to annoy me. I went into the kitchen to make a Cup•A•Soup, when I noticed the soothing in-office music from the speaker above the fridge playing a Royal Philharmonic version of "The Wreck of the *Edmund Fitzgerald*." I remembered the night before. I had to smile at the craziness of it, and then hummed a snatch of the song, when . . .

. . . when the melody line began to see-saw back and forth in my head, note by note, in a stream, like a violin bow across its strings. *No!*

But it was happening. Inside my head I was playing music back and forth. For the first time, I felt socked in the stomach with the knowledge that I had a child, and that a mystery had passed between the two of us, and that no bond on earth could be closer.

I couldn't delete the song from my head. It was like the smell of bacon on a Sunday morning. I went outside and had a quick walk down to the news shop on the corner.

Nothing could weed that wretched tune from my brain.

The legend lives on . . .

From the Chippewa on down . . .

. . . nwod no aweppihC eht morF

. . . no sevil dnegel ehT

I went into the stairwell, concrete and ugly, but with gorgeous operatic acoustics. I began singing the song backwards and forwards. My armpits felt cold. I was so confused. I ran down to the underground parking lot and hopped into my car. My chest was heaving, my head felt overinflated. I put on the radio to find a song to replace "The Wreck of the *Edmund Fitzgerald*." Petula Clark's "Downtown." I switched it off, and then it too began to play in reverse in my head.

I ran red lights all the way home, parked the car diagonally on the street and ran upstairs. I walked into the apartment, and Jeremy was sanding away at the kitchen walls with sandpaper wrapped around a sponge. Beside him were two barbecues, a colour TV and a microwave oven, all in their factory boxes.

"Mom! Why are you home so early? I was going to surprise you with a first coat of red."

I said nothing. I walked over to where he was sitting, on a chair beside a radiator. I sat down, and with a force I didn't know I had, I pulled him up and clamped him to my chest.

"Mom?"

"Shut up, Jeremy."

"Mom?"

"You don't have to paint walls any more, Jeremy."

He tried to reply, but I sat on a dining-room chair and pulled him onto my lap. I don't think either of us had any idea what to say. Finally, I began to sing "The Wreck of the *Edmund Fitzgerald*" backwards. I said, "I gave it to you."

"Gave what?"

"The ability to sing backwards. I didn't know it, but today it all came blasting through my head."

"Was that a good thing or a bad thing?"

I'd never held anybody before. People have weight. They're warm. You can feel their heart and lungs pumping from within. I don't know what it was I'd been expecting—a marionette?

Jeremy began to sing the song forwards, but I said, "No need."

I looked over at the kitchen wall. I looked at the paint, and it struck me that between that paint and the kitchen wall there had to be a space of some sort—even if it was a millionth of an inch thick. I tried to imagine being in a microscopic spacecraft, digging into that paint, searching for that secret charmed space. Perhaps it only exists as a concept, but maybe it's real, too. But I suppose to hunt for it is to kill it. You can only feel it surround you, feel it cover you, feel it make you whole.

It's now time to take a very big gulp of air here, to remember that it was seven years ago when all of this happened. It often feels like just a week to me. Time is whimsical and cruel.

This whole story began on that evening I stood in a parking lot outside a video store, when I looked up into the sky and saw my first-ever comet—the ludicrously named Hale-Bopp—and decided I wanted peace, not certainty, in my life.

But now, seven years later, I ask you, what happens when a comet hits the earth? What happens when things stop being cosmic and become something you can hold in your hand in a very real sense? I'm not trying to be coy here. I'm about to describe two events that happened to me just a few days ago, the two events that started me telling this story.

First, on Thursday after work, I found a meteorite, or rather, one found me. What are the chances of *that?* I was walking home from the Mac's Milk, and it was raining slightly—misting. I was maybe a minute from my condo building's front doors, wondering what movie I might watch that night, or which DVD to rent. I heard a hiss and what sounded like an armload of heavy books slapping onto a freshly polished linoleum floor. It was just in front of me, and I jumped in shock, my cantaloupe, cottage cheese and Thai chicken Super Wrap falling onto the sidewalk.

There was a pothole in the road—one just large enough to make you phone city hall to complain. Its edges were uniformly round and crisp. I walked closer. Inside was a little brown rock that was steaming, to be frank, like dog shit on a cold winter day. I thought I had to be imagining this. But I wasn't. But—well, what do any of us feel when something statistically odd occurs?

There were no other pedestrians on the street—mine simply isn't a pedestrian kind of neighbourhood—nor were there any cars or, as I looked to see, anybody looking out onto the street from inside his apartment. This little event was mine, and mine alone.

I bent down and inspected the meteorite more closely. It was the shape and size of a baby's fist, brown and covered with little craters, like an asteroid. I spat on it to see if it would sizzle my spit, but it didn't. I lowered my hand to it and felt its heat, tapping it with my finger, as though testing a recently unplugged iron. I was able to hold it, and quickly picked it up. This sucker was *mine*.

I picked up my scrambled foods, stuck the meteorite into my coat pocket and ran upstairs. I dumped the groceries by the sink, placed the cooling stone on the counter and pulled up a stool, looking at my prize closely, as if it contained a space alien or a Kinder Egg treat. But no—it was just a pocked, dimpled, metallic lump, and that was fine by me.

I ate my cottage cheese and the Thai chicken wrap at the counter. I became paranoid. I didn't want a neighbour with too much free time on her hands phoning city hall and reporting the pothole. The person sent to inspect it might recognize the hole as being meteoric and report it to the planetarium, and before I knew it my prize would be taken away from me and no longer be mine. I decided I needed to fill in the hole.

So, my meteorite and I got into my car and drove to Home Depot. There, I bought a sack of sterilized sand, and back at my building I parked by the curb, looked about for pedestrians—unlikely—and then went and filled in the crater like a small sandbox. Done. Nobody would recognize the hole for what it was. They couldn't.

I crumpled up the empty bag, hucked it into the basement trash bin, then went upstairs, feeling as if I'd just dumped a body in the Fraser River. It felt good, actually. I was in cahoots with the stars themselves.

Concentrating on anything much that night was hard. I couldn't even feel lonely, as every time I began to do so I looked at my stone, and I felt more special than I did lonely—what an odd cure for my problems.

Where had this meteorite been? Was it from some other star? From some *Star Trek* galaxy of people with bad latex forehead prostheses? My own knowledge of our universe isn't broad, but I do know that stars don't shed rocks—they shed energy. Something as dull as a rock had to come from a planet or a moon, most likely one that blew up or got hit by another planet or moon. Poor little planet. Poor little rock.

In any event, before going to bed, I poured myself a glass of Pinot Gris, looked at the lump and took it to my bedroom, where I set it beside my alarm clock. Just before I fell asleep, though, I grabbed my asteroid and placed it under my pillow, like a quarter from the tooth fairy. I remembered how odd it was as a child to receive twenty-five cents for a tooth from the tooth fairy. This guy—I've always thought of the tooth fairy as a guy—he goes into children's bedrooms collecting dead teeth? What—for medical experimentation? Nobody ever tells you what he does with the things. I guess when you're shedding teeth, you're young enough to pretend to go along with your parents' corny ideas. In my mind, the tooth fairy was actually that guy I found beside the railway tracks cut into two, back when I was twelve. If it really was him, he might have been relieved to be dead. I mean, come on, look at his job description.

* * *

The second event began at about three in the morning, with my phone ringing. I'm a medium to light sleeper, so a call in the night didn't give me the adrenalin boost it might give others, but I *do* remember knocking my meteorite to the floor as I answered, and scrambling to pick it up in my left hand before I said hello.

"Oh—hello. I'm sorry, is this Elizabeth Dunn?" It was a man with a German accent, but not a scary one—more like an academic who narrates Discovery Channel documentaries on fossils or Venus flytraps.

"Who's this?"

"I'm sorry. I thought I would get an answering machine."

"Well, you didn't. Who's this?"

"I'm terribly sorry, Miss Dunn. Truly sorry. My name is Rainer Bayer."

I fumbled through my memory in search of a Rainer Bayer, but no go. "It's three in the morning. Who are you, and why are you calling?"

"I'm with the police department—in the city of Vienna."

"Vienna? As in Austria?"

"That is correct."

"Look, you know what? I'm hanging up. If you call me again, I'm siccing the cops on you. Good*bye*." I put down the phone and fell back to sleep, but couldn't. It was no child on the other end, and there was nothing about the call that seemed, on recollection, prankish. Had I been too abrupt?

The phone rang again. I picked it up and said, "Give me your phone number right now, and I'll phone you back."

"But—"

"Now or never."

And so he gave me his number, with country and city codes as well as his extension. In my confusion I used a Chap Stick to write the number on my side table's glass top. In order to read it, I had to turn on the light and lie with my eyes almost level to the surface. I dialed.

"This is Rainer Bayer."

"Why did you wake me in the middle of the night?"

"My apologies. You're listed as a business in your city's on-line phone directory. I thought I would get a machine."

This was correct. William had set me up as a business to save on taxes. I was awake now. "Okay, Officer Bayer, what's this about?"

"Miss Dunn, I'm doing follow-up research into what you would call a 'person of interest' on a case here in Austria."

"I don't know anybody in Austria."

"Not many people do, Miss Dunn. It's a small country."

"How did you find my phone number?"

"I'll explain that shortly, Miss Dunn."

"Go on. Who are we talking about here?"

"Miss Dunn, as a teenager, did you visit the city of Rome with classmates?"

Pause. "Yes. How did you know?"

"Google, Miss Dunn."

"What does this have to do with Austria?"

"Vienna."

"Vienna, then."

"Maybe something, maybe nothing. Miss Dunn, tell me, did you once attend a discotheque with your classmates."

"I did."

"And do you remember some other students there?"

"Yes. They were from Austria. Is that what this is about?"

"Yes, it is, Miss Dunn."

Rainer said nothing, the way police do on TV, but I can out-wait anybody, and after a good fifteen seconds he said, "Is there anything you'd like to tell me, Miss Dunn?"

"You know what? *You* phoned *me,* so either you tell me something right now or I'm going to hang up."

He said, "We have a man here, a Klaus Kertesz, who was also at the discotheque that night. Mr. Kertesz is under investigation for a number of assaults against several women. It is very frustrating for us because, while we suspect him of much, actual evidence is difficult to find."

"How do I fit into this? Or the disco?"

"By accident, Miss Dunn. When Mr. Kertesz was brought in for questioning, the officers, very unprofessionally, threw him into the back of their police car. Mr. Kertesz required many stitches on his forehead, and was given a dose of painkillers which loosened his tongue."

I thought this over. Administering too many painkillers mixed with a dose of sodium pentothal is a very good means of opening closed mouths. I asked, "And so this guy talked about *me?*"

"He did."

"In what way?"

"He called you Queen Elizabeth."

I said nothing.

"He knew you were from Vancouver. He named your high school. That was how we found you. It was very easy, really. Your friends have even posted photos of your trip on-line."

"You're serious?"

"Go to Google and put in ROME DISCO LIZ 1976 HIGH SCHOOL CANADA, Elizabeth. You'll see that a classmate of yours, Scarlet Halley, has a large number of pages devoted to that trip."

"Go on."

"What Mr. Kertesz said to our officers was not a confession, but rather a sort of provocation. Braggadocio."

"He called me Queen Elizabeth?"

"Is that an unflattering thing?"

"Does it matter?" What surprised me is that he remembered me at all. "Why did he say he remembered me?"

"That remains unclear."

Bayer said nothing, another ploy of silence. I followed his lead. I tried listening for crackling or fuzziness on the phone line, but he could have been phoning from next door—the connection was clear as glass.

Bayer said, "So you *do* remember him, then."

"There were many boys there that night. How do I know which one was him?"

"We could send you jpegs."

"That would be simple enough. But what is it you think he did to me?"

"We were hoping you might be able to tell us, Miss Dunn."

"I'm sorry, but this is bizarre, your phoning in the middle of the night with this bizarre news. Look at it from my point of view."

"I understand, Miss Dunn. Again, I apologize for the awkward time of this call. I was merely going to leave a message."

"Mr. Bayer, do you also have my e-mail address?"

"Actually, no."

"It's eleanorrigby@arctic.ca. 'Eleanor Rigby' is all one word."

"As in the Beatles song?"

"Yes. Eleanorrigby."

"I'll send the images right now."

"What if I do look at this guy's photo and I remember him—what then?"

"We'll cross that bridge when we get to it, Miss Dunn."

My maternal instincts made me keep my cards close to my chest. "Well, I don't know what it is you're expecting me to say, but send along whatever you have and we'll go from there."

"Of course."

I had the distinct impression Bayer knew I was holding back on something, but he had what I suppose you'd call courtly European manners, and left things as they stood. I told him that I'd go boot up my machine and wait for the images to come through. And so I did.

* * *

Even the most random threads of life always knit together in the end.

For example, I remember how, on the flight back from Rome, Scarlet Halley had a powerful anxiety attack just after our captain told us we were passing over Reykjavik, Iceland. She started breathing like a horse after it's broken its leg, knowing instinctively that it's curtains. I'd never seen something like this before, and was interested in what was happening.

The flight attendant whisked Scarlet away to behind the blue cloth that separates business class from proletariat class. They couldn't spot Mr. Burden—he was somewhere in the smoking section downing rye—so I came along out of curiosity, and was able to tell the flight crew a few basic facts about our trip. I remember the smell of the toilet disinfectant, the smell of meals being heated, and the clinking, heavy drinks trolley. Scarlet was leaning against the door with the big handle on it—the one you use if you're going to parachute out with a duffle bag full of hundred-dollar bills. Lucky for Scarlet, there was a doctor on board who plied her with pills, and she floated her way back home.

Later, she turned out to be one of the pregnant girls, but I don't think that had anything to do with her in-flight anxiety attack. We were over Hudson Bay when I figured that maybe Scarlet had been on the brink of a flip-out all through the trip, and it was only once she knew, on a deep level, that she was safe and headed homeward that her body allowed her to unravel. I think that's how our bodies work. Just look at January 1, 2000—all of those elderly people who'd been barely keeping it together for the big December 31, 1999 hurrah suddenly began dropping like flies. I think we all have it within ourselves to hold on just that little bit longer. That's not quite Scarlet's case, but the analogy holds.

I mention this incident as a means of saying that it wasn't until Jeremy came to live with me that he began to go downhill quickly. Maybe I'm flattering myself, but I don't think so. Immediately after his first afternoon bowling with Donna, he came home, sat down on the couch and said to me, "I think something's going wrong."

"Where?"

"With me."

"Why? What is it?"

"I feel . . . fluey."

"Did you take your meds today?"

"No. I felt too good to take them."

"Lie down."

There was a bad summer cold making the rounds that year, and I was hoping that's all it was as I cut up small triangular tuna sandwiches with their crusts removed, *just a cold.*

"How was bowling?"

"It's more fun as an idea than as an actual activity."

"Did you win?" It dawned on me that I didn't know how you won at bowling. Touchdowns? Home runs?

Jeremy said, "It's not so much about winning as it is about renting shoes and drinking slushies."

"Did Donna like it?"

"I don't know. She was smothering me with kindness, the way people do when you're their official sick person."

"Hmm. I'm sure she means well." I vowed to keep my mouth shut about Donna. "Will you see her again?"

"I doubt it. I'm not kidding, I really *do* think she just wants me to be sick so she can nurse me."

We ate sandwiches, and I thought Jeremy was getting better, but when we were almost finished he said, "Uh-oh," and laid himself down on the sofa. His eyes were focused on something far away.

"Jeremy, are you okay? Jeremy?"

He was. He said, "I'm seeing the farmers."

"Are you comfortable? Do you need a blanket?" I got him a pillow.

"Yes, I see the farmers."

"You do? What are they doing?" I have to apologize on behalf of my mortal soul here—I obviously felt awful that he was sick, but a part of me said *Hurrah!* to see Jeremy recapturing his visions.

"We're back on the road, back when the woman's voice told them they'd been forsaken. The road is dusty. Rabbits out in the fields are scurrying into their holes. The birds have vanished. The farmers feel confounded. They've fallen to their knees and are praying for some sort of sign to tell them they haven't been abandoned by the voice."

"Are they getting a sign?"

Jeremy was flat, his arms to his sides, as if jumping off a cliff into water. "Yes—they are."

"What is it?"

"It's not what they'd hoped for. There's a string coming down to them from the sky."

"A string? What's it attached to in the sky?"

"I don't know. Wait—it's more like a rope. And it's tied to something, just a few steps ahead of them on the road. The farmers are walking toward it."

"What's on the end?"

"A bone."

This was creepy. I felt like the shadow of a plane had just flown over me.

"It's one of those freakish bones—a collarbone, with a flat bit and a pointy part. There's another bone coming down from the sky on a rope—a pelvic bone. And now there are more strings, all of these . . . bones. The bones are all clattering together, like wind chimes."

"Are you frightened?"

"No."

"Are the farmers frightened?"

"They are. They're backing away from the bones. They've had their message. They're completely forsaken, and they're in the wilderness now. They're no longer humans—they're dolls or scarecrows or mannequins. Their only salvation lies in placing their faith in the voice who's forsaken them."

This was Jeremy's final vision. Bits of things emerged here and there, but this is the one story that I think really was a story, and it frustrates me not to know what happened to those farmers.

"Do you want some crackers? Some soup later on, maybe?"

"That sounds good."

"I'm going to pop out to the store. I'll be back in a few minutes."

That night we upgraded the cold to flu status. By sunrise Monday morning he became severely bronchial, and by lunch I drove him to the hospital, amid traffic that reminded me of my cubicle at Landover Communication Systems.

The hospital admitted Jeremy, plopped him into a bed and then literally vacuumed out muck from his lungs. I can still clearly see the almost bored look on the nurse's face, as if she were cleaning the den. I'd never been around a sick person before, and I wondered if maybe appearing bored was the most comforting pose to strike with a patient. In any event, I knew that I was going to take time off work and phoned Liam to tell him.

I then went to the gift shop, bought a stack of magazines and gum, and went upstairs and sat beside him there. He became clear-headed near day's end. He said, "Oh crap. I'm *here* again."

"Sorry about that."

He glowered at the room as if he'd been kept at school for detention, then looked at me. "How bad is it?"

"They don't know if it's a cold or flu, but it led to pneumonia, and now you're here."

Again he looked around the room, then up at the ceiling. "The mattress here is too firm, and it could use a four-inch foam underlay. And I don't know what they spray it with to keep it sanitary from patient to patient."

I said, "At least it folds upward."

"I forgot about that. Where's the button?" It was by his side and I gave it to him. Like William with his old Hot Wheels set, Jeremy started messing with his bed. "Now *this* is a mattress."

I said, "Actually, Jeremy, it's a total sleep system."

"When I get out of here, I'm going to sell to institutions. That's where the big money is."

"Really, now?"

"Yes. My small and manageable dream has just become slightly larger."

* * *

An hour later, Jeremy fell unconscious, and he stayed that way for a few days, wandering in and out of a fevered blur. He looked at me, but I'm still not sure if he recognized me, which was horrible.

By the next weekend he was able to come home, but his motor skills had largely deteriorated. He shook, he froze, and even using a spoon could quickly become hard work. I had to locate the balance between mothering him and babying him, as well as learn how to treat him both as my son and as a man.

A few days after this, Jeremy relapsed—one evil rancid sponge-mop in a whorehouse of an armpit of a gorilla of an every-loathsome-metaphor-in-the-book flu. I spent my days in the condo, drying Jeremy's forehead from his sweats, doing all those things I was told, as a child, good nurses do. It required almost no training; the instinct must be built into us the way birds know how to build nests.

Caring for people is so odd—it's boring but it's not boring at all. It's like being in a house and you hear a funny noise and you freeze, ears cocked, wondering if you'll hear the funny noise again—except with a sick person you're always in that frozen state of mind, attuned to the tiniest change in your patient's condition.

At one point Jeremy attempted a lacklustre stroke or two of paint on the red kitchen wall, but I commanded him back to bed.

During clear patches, he tried to rest my mind by asking silly questions.

"Mom, why does water have no taste?"

"Because we're made of water, that's why."

"Mom, why does having money feel so good?"

"Because . . ." I was stumped. Why *does* it make us feel so good?

Jeremy said, "Mom, you don't strike me as the type to get a thrill from spending money."

"Me? No. But I'm not dumb—it gives me security. An unmarried woman of my age has to have that, no matter what her place is in the world."

"But haven't you ever just taken a wad of dough and splurged on something completely useless but great?"

"Like what?"

"I don't know. Chinchilla underwear. An exotic dancer who makes you flaming crepes and then undresses you with his tongue."

"No."

"You should do something. If I wasn't such a waste case, I'd happily be spending your money for you."

"Don't be so negative. You're not a waste case, and I'd be happy to help you spend my money."

Actually, I downplayed things earlier. I *do* have lots of money tucked away. My salary is large, I don't spend it and I play the market, where I tend to follow my hunches and almost always win. It's just common sense, most of it. In the early 1990s I bought twenty stocks because their names contained the word *micro*. Since I sold them at the right time, that decision alone secured my retirement. At the same time, you also have to buy stocks in companies that make soup and toothpaste, because no matter what happens to the economy, people will always need them.

To be more precise, I'm *rich,* and it actually *is* odd that I don't splurge on myself, ever. But when you're alone, you know that money is the one thing that can keep you safe. Safe from what? Safe from being hauled away in the middle of the night and baked into protein wafer cookies to feed people who are in relationships. Safe from worrying about being eighty and entering a rest-home bidding war with some other rich person over who's going to change my diaper that afternoon. A rich man is always simply a rich man, but a rich woman is only a poor woman who just happens to have money. I said, "Actually, I do use my money—to keep my family in check."

"How?"

"To be blunt, who's in my will and who isn't. It's cheesy and low-class, but it's power, and I do like it. If I was whacked by a bus tomorrow, there'd be a minimum of fuss followed by a gleeful reading of my will."

"You're being too harsh on yourself."

"The one exception would be Mother. She has no financial interest in me, but she'd be itching to see who snagged what."

There was a silence.

I said, "Needless to say, my son, your arrival has altered things."

"Ralph Lauren makes iron lungs?"

* * *

Back to a week ago. Back to me walking into my living room, deep in the night, checking my e-mail and seeing Herr Bayer's message with an icon telling me of an attachment. Back to me breathing in and out a few times before clicking the download button.

I knew what I was going to see, and after twenty endless seconds what I saw was the Viennese person of interest, Klaus Kertesz, the obvious father of Jeremy—older, hairier and more European-looking in that way you can't ever really articulate—but it was him. I must have been very drunk indeed that night at the Roman nightclub to forget that face. On seeing it, I felt like I'd fallen and bumped my head on the butcher block. My ears stung.

I'm not even sure if it was good news or bad news to see the face of Klaus Kertesz before me. He's Jeremy's father, and yet he's—well, a rapist or molester or who knows what. The only thing that made sense to me was to go fetch my lucky meteorite, my message from above; and I've been holding it ever since.

Indeed, a week has now passed, and I haven't yet phoned Herr Bayer, nor have I e-mailed him a proper reply. I've skipped work, and I've been sitting by my computer, writing these words while toying with the face of Klaus Kertesz, making him thinner, younger, more like Jeremy. I keep looking at framed photos of my son—it's so hard to see my own face in there somewhere. I feel like that one Scrabble tile that has no letter on it. I'm a Styrofoam puff used in packaging. I'm a napkin at McDonald's. I'm invisible tape. Lucky Prince William, to be able to see his mother so clearly in his own face.

* * *

I've not mentioned my family's involvement in Jeremy's care—or Donna's. I thought they'd be at the condo often, but once the novelty wore off, the pace of their visits slowed. There was one funny moment with William, on the phone, when he said, "I have to do due diligence here, Lizzie: any chance Junior is a gold digger?"

"He's going to stick my head in a plastic Wonder Bread bag for my cheesy condo? *Please.*"

"You can never tell."

"William, a new BMW isn't going to happen. Maybe a shiny bauble or a trinket. I don't know. I've never had someone to spend money on before. It's new territory for me."

An hour later, the phone rang. It was Leslie. "What's this I hear about you buying expensive jewellery for Jeremy?"

Mother was a terrible caregiver. "Whenever you kids were sick, I'd lock you outside for a few hours and you'd be good as new. Just stick him in some cold fresh air." She meant well, but she had no tolerance for the ever-worsening, intractable manifestations of the disease. She *did* want desperately to introduce Jeremy to her friends, but was slow in doing so as it meant revealing my shameful teen pregnancy. She toyed with the idea of "the long-lost nephew," but William, Leslie and I scotched the notion.

In the end she brought along her easily bullied friend Sheila. During her visit, the woman asked no questions about Jeremy's past; I can only imagine the sugar-coated version of the truth Mother fed her. Jeremy, of course, was charming, and for the first time I felt that Mother might be proud of me. The sensation was so new and jarring that I had to go into my bedroom, close the door, and sit there to both analyze and savour the novelty. When I returned to the living room, Jeremy was opening some of the boxloads of gifts Mother had brought him—pricey designer stuff. Mother's not a cheap woman, but nor is she extravagant. I suspect she was trying to buy her way out of guilt, but I kept that to myself, and Jeremy was no dummy—he would have figured that out in a blink.

Later, he asked, "Growing up, was your mother cheap with you?"

"No. Not really." Actually, Mother may have taken some sort of pride in my perceived virginity, but she was also always trying to tart me up in overpriced designer gear and makeup—anything to boost my sex appeal. *Make the boys interested in taking you down off the shelf for a look.* If I'd shown even a sneeze worth of interest, a leather dominatrix outfit and a set of handcuffs could have been mine—anything for a show of interest in sex. And if you forced her to choose between Liz as virgin and Liz as tramp, my hunch is that she'd have chosen the latter. Fortunately, Leslie was a far more enthusiastic participant in Mother's campaign of sex.

* * *

Jeremy was right about Donna: in a brief time she was all over the condo like a teenager lining up for concert tickets. Not to disparage her intentions, but she converted one afternoon of bowling into a life partnership with the man. I'd taken a leave of absence from work and so extra help wasn't needed. Some conversation might have been nice, but when Donna visited, her focus on Jeremy was so intense it reminded me of stalker movies.

"He's suffering."

"He's just sleeping."

"Imagine the *pain.*"

"It's actually the opposite. He goes numb."

In her eyes I was branded a witch.

After a week of this, Jeremy said, "This is going to get sexual really soon, trust me. She's a control freak, and I'm a control freak's dream date—to be more precise, I'm her prisoner. She has to go. What can we do about it?"

"Best we simply tell her to stop."

"You be the one to do it. She'll go ballistic."

And she *did*. It was ugly and boring, and I was accused of being unappreciative, and Jeremy was accused of faking his illness for attention, and . . . Even thinking about her gets my blood to boiling. Once you see a person go psycho, you can never look at him or her the same way again. You hear that so-and-so's crazy and it's cute and funny, but once you've seen it for real, it's over.

The day after the outburst, Liam visited around dinnertime. "Donna was very upset."

Jeremy said, "She's psycho." It was a good health day for Jeremy, and to look in from the outside you'd never know he was falling apart.

Liam knew enough to leave the Donna issue alone. "I've got three of my choir friends in the car downstairs. Can I invite them up to hear Jeremy sing?"

This was such a shameless and unexpected request, we were happy to have them up, two women and a man. They were polite and quiet, and for once I had things to serve guests besides pudding cups and ouzo. One of the women had brought a tape recorder with her, and she was timid about using it, but she had no need to be. She asked Jeremy, "Can you sing classically?"

"I can, but I don't know any of the theory behind it—just the sounds."

"That's okay."

"What would you like me to sing backwards? Remember, I max out at around thirty seconds."

"Actually, we've made a list . . ." Indeed they had. We spent two hours recording music. For a few of the pieces, Liam asked us to speak during Jeremy's singing, only to prove to listeners that this wasn't a stunt.

The four of them left, and that was that.

* * *

Some scraps of paper I just found . . .

A new order, cold white lights that burn and die.

—

A tornado with a halo

—

A guy throwing a thrashing body in the trunk of a Chevy

—

A 747 the size and shape of a hotel, flying to Jerusalem, with stacking chairs instead of seats

* * *

The police ultimately learned who it was who chopped the man in half in the 1970s. It was the conductor, Ben, the one who'd been so upset about seeing the body—as well as the man who gave me a ride home from the PGE station. Who could possibly seem more innocent than the guy who found him? It was some sort of sex thing that went horribly wrong, but then with Ben it turned out things had gone horribly wrong with three other unlucky souls. He was serial material.

The reason Ben was so annoyed with me that afternoon, he confessed, is that he wanted the body to be a bit more far gone before it was discovered. Stupid man. If he wanted nobody to find the body, he should have carried the bits into the tunnel a quarter-mile or so away.

I thought of the body, and I thought of Jeremy when I first saw him in the hospital—the sense of miraculousness that coloured both experiences. I decided to visit the tracks again. Maybe the aura of the place would trigger something inside me, make me remember that night on the Roman roof. It couldn't hurt.

I drove out to Horseshoe Bay—it was a gorgeous day—parked and then climbed up onto the railway tracks. They looked and smelled exactly as I remembered. I liked that timelessness. I picked a switch of baby alder, just like the one I used to probe the corpse. I walked to the spot where the corpse had been, but there was nothing there to mark the end of the man's life, not even a sun-faded plastic daisy or two sticks made into a cross.

I walked along a bit further. The blackberries were out and the birds were making the most of them. There seemed to be less litter along the tracks than in the old days, but other than that, it could easily have been the 1970s.

I tried, but no memories of that night in Rome came back to me. No gangbang. No molestation. I was as honest with myself as I could be; if I could deny an entire pregnancy, denying a rape might be equally as plausible. But no.

I heard a noise, which I knew was one of those tiny speeder cars the railway uses for small errands. I moved off the tracks and stood in a small patch of sun-baked plantain and native geranium. The speeder slowed down and the man driving it said something into his mobile communication device, and then said to me, "Hey, you can't walk here. It's private property."

"Really?"

"Haven't you heard of September eleventh?"

I rolled my eyes.

"I'll call the cops."

"You do that."

We both knew this conversation was doomed. He left and I walked back to the car. Something about the exchange made me make up my mind. Here's what I'm going to do: I've booked a flight to Vienna for tomorrow, via Frankfurt, first class—moneybags me. I've also forwarded my arrival time to Herr Bayer. My stomach feels fizzy; my head feels like mist. My heart is heavy, with either gold or lead—I can't really tell which.

A final thought before I leave: A few years ago I decided that I was going to make a list of all the things I'm not very good at, and then stop doing them—fixing the paper jams in the office; trying to understand how my car works; the logic behind Miss America pageants. I thought this decision would streamline my life, make it better—and up to a point it did. But I realize now that by deciding not to do things,

I've lost millions of threads of chance and opportunity to have new experiences, to meet new people—to be alive, really. So I'm going to start doing things I'm bad at again. Heck, I'm going to do things I've never even *tried.*

* * *

Okay.

I'm writing these words from a German prison cell, located, I think, in the town of Morfelden, somewhere outside of Frankfurt. On the way here somebody opened the door of the van, and that's what I saw on the road sign outside. I've spent the past three hours in solitary confinement, which must surely be some sort of cosmic joke, as I've spent most of my life in solitary confinement. How, one might ask, did this happen?

The prison isn't as bad as I'd imagined prisons to be—no tattooed prisoners slashing their wrists and spritzing blood at guards, no squalid cell with built-up layers of puke, shit, pornography and razor blades. It's actually white and spotless in here, maybe the size of my bedroom back home. There's no easy way of knowing what time of day it is, and it's wonderfully quiet. I can think of far worse punishments than a German solitary prison cell. Even the food isn't too bad—three hours and they've already fed me cabbage, wurst, green vegetables—and the staff here are quite friendly to me.

I'll here recount the steps to my prison cell. After I'd booked my flight to Vienna, calmness fell over my life, the kind that descends after making a huge decision, the calm that's the opposite of remorse. The Dwarf and all the ditherers at the offices of Landover Communication Systems were offhandedly cheerful when I told them I was going to Austria. While I've only been gone a short while, I'm sure that my work cubicle has already been absorbed into all the others, leaving no traces of my existence there. Had my co-workers known the odd circumstances of my trip, about this Klaus Kertesz, the gossip factor would have been higher, but my secret was like my meteorite: sharing it with others would devalue it.

I also didn't tell my family the true reason for my trip. Why would I? Me doing something out of the ordinary would be interesting to them for about two minutes and then be just another piece of noise in their lives. But my secret isn't part of that noise—it's all mine.

I'll admit it, once the shock of buying my ticket subsided, I drove across town and spent a fair whack on an image makeover at one of the city's more expensive salons. All to no good. Even as they saw me approach, I could tell they were scurrying into the back room, where they drew straws to see who would have to work on me. To their credit, they did try, but I am beauty-proof. My efforts at renovating my wardrobe years ago with Jeremy never went far; there's just no point. I'm a nice, clean, well-shod, well-dressed blank. I'm not even someone in a crowd scene in a movie. The director would yell, "Stop! Haul that woman out of there! She's too blank even for a crowd scene!"

I must also here comment on the difference between flying to Europe on a 747 charter in 1976 and flying there in 2004 in first class on Lufthansa's craft the *Schleswig-Holstein. Me,* climbing up that little staircase into the bubble—endless leg room, delicious foods and a wide selection of film, TV and documentaries. I can see why the ruling class wants to keep the underclass far away. The proles would rampage if they saw how dishy life is up in the bubble. My one complaint is the little map they displayed overhead that showed us exactly where the plane was, the outside temperature, the estimated time of arrival. It made me feel like my life was in miniature. It was like watching the seconds tick by until, as Jeremy and Pink Floyd both pointed out to me, I was shorter of breath and one day closer to death. Or, as Jeremy said, "Well, at least when you sing it backwards, it's one day closer to being born."

* * *

A Ms. Greenaway from the Canadian government was just here, asking if conditions in the prison are adequate. She's the only person I've been able to speak with so far.

"Adequate? I could happily live here."

"There's no need for sarcasm, Ms. Dunn. My job is to ensure you're being treated properly."

"I'm not being sarcastic. This place is okay." I didn't mention my lifelong belief that we, as humans, are a wretched species indeed, and deserving of harsh punishments for the crimes we casually get away with in our daily lives.

The quality of Ms. Greenaway's silence assured me she knew I wasn't joking. We were seated in a cubic white room with a window the size of a playing card, and I could tell it was night outside. I scanned the floor for scuffing or stains or anything remotely biological, but found nothing.

"Ms. Greenaway, could you please tell me why it is I'm in jail here?"

"Oh *please.*"

"Really."

Her eyes told me she considered me an idiot. "You don't know?"

"No."

After more telltale silence Ms. Greenaway said, "Well, I'm not going to be the one to tell you. It isn't my role."

"That's okay."

She was huffy. "You mean you *truly* have no idea why you're here?"

"Do I have to repeat myself? No, I don't."

Ms. Greenaway was losing patience. "I need names of people to contact. Family. Friends."

"I don't have any friends." I considered my family. If my family members were to be contacted, there'd be a scene, a bad one, one that could easily be prevented. "I have a brother, William. He travels for a living. Contact him on his cellphone. His wife is an idiot. Neither you nor I want her involved in this." I gave her William's number and asked her what happens next.

She shrugged. She was obviously considering her best interest here. "Someone will be here in the morning to work with you."

"Will they tell me why I'm here?"

"I can't say that."

"Oh, for goodness' sake, Ms. Greenaway, I'm not a pinhead. You know exactly what I went through in the terminal, and so does everybody there. There has to have been a good reason for it."

"It's not my place to discuss this. I'm sorry. Goodbye."

With Donna-like efficiency she vanished, and I'm happy to report I felt no fear or worry at her vanishing. To have all ifs and buts of life stripped away—to have everything thought out for you every day and minute of your life—prison is the opposite of freedom, and, as such, is almost as liberating. I can't tell you.

Maybe it was that tiny patch of night sky I saw outside the window while speaking with Ms. Greenaway, but suddenly I'm sleepy. Good night.

* * *

I'm not emphasizing enough Jeremy's worries about his visions leaving him. After he fell from the clouds and landed on my sofa, in between his fevers, we'd sing rock anthems backwards together—or we'd simply watch that wretched wasteland known as daytime TV.

Time was a touchy subject with Jeremy. Life is finite; Jeremy's was simply more finite than most. If nothing else, you get used to being alive.

I sometimes think that having visions is a way of inserting yourself into the future you suspect you're never going to have. People who see the world coming to an end are simply people who can't imagine life after they die. If they have to go, they're going to take the world along with them.

All that being said, the farmers did exercise their pull on me. One afternoon I visited the library and for Jeremy borrowed books on farming. A silly notion, but one that pleased Jeremy no end. "I was always stuck with farm families, but they never put me to work that way. Funny, because farming is something I might actually enjoy doing."

"Really?"

"Oh *yeah*. A few acres—putting seeds in the ground—watching them grow, flower, bear fruit, turn to soil come fall—I could be so happy doing just that."

"Would you miss the city?"

"No. I don't think so."

"You wouldn't find it dull?"

"Nope. Plants make you think of next year. I think that's why I see the farmers: they have no choice but to think of next year."

I confess here that farming has always baffled me—its monotony, the fact that a good farm, properly maintained, ought really never to change from one century to the next. It's like the opposite of time travel. And imagine going to all that work, work, work, and there's never a moral to it. No plot. No *eureka!* Just food production and *days*. And weather.

Jeremy said, "Yup, I really want to be a farmer."

I kept mum, remembering William at the family's most recent Easter dinner. He was boozed up and discussing the future career paths of his two TV-soaked rats. "Only losers make decisions when things are bad. The time to rejig your life is the time when it's seemingly smooth. Use your brief moments of calm to leverage yourself into a next place that's just as good." William obviously believes suffering doesn't make people better, only different. I disagree, but kept my mouth shut.

* * *

I suppose it's morning; I've no idea how long I slept. What a cruel wrinkle it is to stick a jet-lagged person into a time-proof room. I suppose I'll have to figure out the time of day based on the sugar content of the meals they insert through my door. Extra sugar means morning.

As there's nothing else to do, I'll continue with my travel journal.

Okay: landing.

Everything seemed normal as we circled the airport. I found myself surprisingly giddy to be on the Continent again, and like most tourists arriving in Europe, I goose-necked out the windows to see the world beneath the wings. Unlike North American landscapes, European landscapes, viewed through an airplane window, resemble well-drawn maps.

Walking up the jet ramp into the terminal, I immediately knew it was a baking hot afternoon in Frankfurt. Almost as quickly, I could tell that the terminal's interior had minimal air conditioning to combat the heat.

We hiked for ten minutes to Immigration, which quickly processed us. Once into the terminal proper, I asked a staffer which gate held my flight to Vienna. I was told to check the screen every fifteen minutes for updates—a computer malfunction in the morning had slowed down the airport's control towers, and the domino effect delayed almost all subsequent flights. People who normally might not be flustered found their resolve vanishing as they fanned themselves with scuffed boarding cards and sweat-smudged copies of the *International Herald Tribune*. The men were growing stubble, while the women had shiny skin. It seemed as if every junior soccer team on earth was being routed through Frankfurt. Young people were sleeping in every nook and corner. It was as if the airport's designers looked into coach class and said, "Hey! Let's create the architectural version of this!" Shame on the airlines.

Fortunately, I had access to the first-class lounge. Through a sleek aluminum door into a haven of refrigerated pleasures—plush furniture, silk fabric walls that loaned the space a muted silence, trays of sandwiches as might be found at a wedding, and a large, polished chrome bar. It became very easy to forget the cattle herds outside. I took a shower, put on a new blouse and tried to forget that I'd been up for almost twenty-four hours. I sat on a lovely plush sofa and nibbled at a ham sandwich from the food area. That was when I noticed all of the police and fire vehicles flooding the Tarmac. Even someone who's spent almost no time in airports could tell that something was up. Like everybody else, visions of terrorism filled my mind.

Wait . . .

A hard-boiled egg, a chocolate cookie and a plastic cup with room-temperature coffee have arrived in my cell. Tea time?

* * *

So, as I was noting, the Tarmac swarmed with emergency vehicles, while an internal alarm sounded in the hallways outside the lounge. We in the lounge stood up, stared at each other as if we knew each other, and then looked to the attractive young man and woman at the lounge's door. They were obviously unaccustomed to what was happening, and were fielding phone calls while shielding their other ear from the general din.

German instructions boomed from speakers cocooned within the silk walls. An older couple bolted for the lounge's door, but the two staffers at the desk blocked them, using their bodies as barricades, saying that it was safer to remain inside.

"Let us out." The would-be escapees were Americans, obviously retirees.

"No. We have been instructed that you are safer here in this lounge."

I'm sure the word went like a nail through everybody's brain. *Safer?*

"What's happening out there?"

"We are not at liberty to tell you." Even under duress, the Germans used perfect English.

A crowd formed at the door. The first man, the American, brushed past the airline's counter woman and opened the door just enough for us inside to witness a mass evacuation through the sliver crack in the door: squeals and charging masses of travellers running as if from a Terminator. The American man said, "Holy—" before a black leather glove came down on his carotid, while another set of gloves pushed him back into the lounge anteroom. I saw the black barrels of several rifles.

Outside the lounge window, an Aer Lingus 767 and a LanChile craft were being evacuated using wheeled dollies and yellow inflatable slides. Strange reaction, but I thought the slides looked like fun. Mercedes vans, of which there were now nearly a hundred, were whisking people away from the vicinity of the lounge. Everything seemed to involve taking people away from where *we* were. The wife of the American man was hysterical and tried to break the triple-glazed windows with a blond maple chair. I went to stop her and, as I did, saw sharpshooters on the terminal's roof.

That was when a team of twenty men in riot police gear, armed with Kevlar shields and flanked by four German shepherds, smashed in through the lounge doors. They charged directly at me, and judo-chopped me in my own carotid artery. I fell to the floor, whereupon my hands were bound behind my back with plastic strip handcuffs. I was hog-tied and carried outside into the emptied terminal. I had no idea what any of the men were saying, but they were in German military outfits and didn't seem in the least like terrorists. They were well organized and superbly trained.

The whole sequence, from my first biting into my sandwich up to total evacuation of the airport and my capture, was maybe five minutes. Aside from the melodramatic judo chop to my carotid and that first minute or so that I was hog-tied, the German police or soldiers, or whatever they were, were gentlemanly. Nobody said a word as they marched me out of Terminal Two, abandoned travel gear everywhere—carry-on bags, baby carriers, designer shopping bags, lunches, datebooks. I remember one of those little blue carts that senior citizens ride on. It had been hastily shoved into an alcove near a currency exchange booth, bleeping away. One of the Germans went over and smacked it on the dashboard, at which point the silence in the terminal was complete.

We marched out into the Foreign Arrivals traffic area, where there were no cars, and where the heat was crinkling the airport's buildings into desert visions. There was no traffic noise, and there were no planes visible or audible in the sky, or any wind. We might as well have been in a Manitoba wheat field.

I was shown into an armoured van, a soldier on each side of me and three opposite me. None of them said a word. After a few minutes of driving, someone knocked from the front and we stopped. Another soldier was added to our vehicle, and that's when I saw the sign saying Morfelden.

A few minutes later we pulled into a garage, where I was escorted to my solitary confinement cell. I did the math: from the ham sandwich to solitary confinement took inside of a half-hour.

And aside from the jittery Ms. Greenaway, that's the story of my incarceration. I was responsible for the total evacuation of one of the world's biggest airports in the middle of the day during peak travel season. Me!

* * *

I've watched enough TV crime shows and movies to know what was coming next: a brightly lit interrogation room. One man interviewed me while five other men, their roles unknown to me, watched from their positions along the rear wall. The only thing that was different from TV or film was a platter of gingerbread cookies atop a paper doily resting on a little table.

My interrogator was a thin man who seemed more like a psychologist than a cop or military person. I asked him his name: Mr. Schroeder. I asked him, "Are you with the government? How do I know you're not terrorists posing as cops?"

"You have too much imagination, Miss Dunn."

"I have no such thing. My life is practical. I like practical things."

"Do you know why you're being detained here, Miss Dunn?"

"No."

Mr. Schroeder seemed almost bored. "Miss Dunn, what do you do in Canada?"

"I work at a place called Landover Communication Systems. I sit in an Aeron chair and spend my days pushing electrons around with a stick."

This baffled him, but then he understood me. "A joke?"

"No. The joke is always on me."

"You were going to Vienna, Miss Dunn. May I ask why *Vienna?*"

I thought about this question. To answer it correctly would mean telling him the story of my life. It would mean revealing to the world the truth about Jeremy's father. I felt like one of those Hollywood actresses who refuses to name the father of her children. I said, "I thought Vienna would be a pretty place to go—a place very different from home."

"You chose it at random?"

"Yes. No. I had my wisdom teeth removed years ago, and I watched *The Sound of Music* on painkillers. It really changed me."

"There is no need to be facetious, Miss Dunn."

"I'm not being facetious, Mr. Schroeder. Phone my dentist."

"Miss Dunn, just so you know, the Canadian government has complied with our request that we interview every person in your family, their friends and their friends'

friends. We will be interviewing your co-workers, your neighbours, and searching your apartment—with all of its documents and all of your computer files. There is nothing about you that we won't know by the end of this."

"There's nothing to know about me. My life is boring."

"We both know that's not true, Miss Dunn."

Once they sniffed through my phone records, they'd find Herr Bayer's call, and that would be it. I figured I might as well keep them hanging; for once, I had power. I said, "I think you're threatening me, and I resent that. I'm a peaceful person. You tell me more about what's happening here or I go mute on you."

"Did you pack your bags yourself, Miss Dunn?"

"Of course I did."

"Did you leave them anywhere with any one person, even if only for a minute?"

"They asked me that at check-in in Vancouver. No."

"Did you fly here alone?"

"Yes."

"Were you supposed to meet with anybody on your trip to Frankfurt?"

"No."

"Were you to meet with anybody in Vienna?"

A fraction of a pause, followed by, "No."

"I think you're not telling me the full story, Miss Dunn."

"Mr. Schroeder, you're not telling me the full story, either."

"One moment, Miss Dunn."

I was left alone in the interrogation room. I stared at the cookies on the plate on the doily. Had the Germans now invented truth cookies? Did they think I'd be tempted because of my size? I looked away. Then I felt tired—jet lag. The dreamlike trip through the abandoned airport. The white cell. I just wanted to close my eyes.

Mr. Schroeder came back in with two men, one of whom was dressed in North American clothing, a noticeable difference. "This is Mr. Brace. He is from your government."

I nodded.

"And this is someone whose name you need not know for now. He is German."

Another nod.

Mr. Brace said, "Miss Dunn, you know that you shut down the world's seventh busiest airport?"

"So I hear."

"You cost the local economy tens of millions of dollars."

"And?"

"To be frank, the Germans are very pissed off with you."

"And me with them. I was eating a ham sandwich and wondering if I should read the complimentary copy of *The Economist* when suddenly they assaulted me and tied me up like a pig at a luau." I'd just used the words *ham* and *pig* in the same sentence. Of all things, I wondered if that was politically correct, to allow so much meat in one sentence.

"Miss Dunn, let me ask you, a week ago last Thursday, in Vancouver, were you out for a walk around, say, 5:40 in the afternoon?"

What? My meteorite? "That's just a meteorite in my luggage—a stupid rock. Why the hell would it send an entire airport into lockdown mode? Good *Lord*. It's just a rock."

The two men looked at each other in a way I didn't like.

I said, "What—it's against the law to carry meteorites? The earth is hit with millions of them every day. I checked on Google."

Mr. Brace said, "Miss Dunn, what you found wasn't a meteorite."

"Oh."

"Miss Dunn, your meteorite is a chunk of the fuel core from an RTG, a Radioisotopic Thermoelectric Generator. It powered a Soviet-era Cosmos satellite. The unit came apart in space, and we know the trajectory of its constituent parts—across the Pacific between the Aleutian Islands and the Alaska–B.C. coast between 5:39 and 5:40. I guess we underestimated its fall."

"I see."

"German authorities found this highly radioactive core inside your bag during a standard luggage X-ray. They assumed it was a component in a dirty bomb. You can see why people might have been alarmed."

"Okay." There was a silence. "Can I go now, then?"

"Not quite. We have to have a lab confirm a spectral analysis of the fuel. It's a formality. We want to confirm that it's part of a batch milled in 1954 in a Soviet secret city called Arzamas-16."

"Fair enough." I decided to make small talk, which always sends men running from me. "You must be relieved it wasn't a dirty bomb, then. All you had to do was ask me what was in the suitcase. You didn't need to put me in jail."

"Standard procedure, Miss Dunn."

We spoke of technicalities for a few minutes. I again asked if it was time to return to the prison.

"Yes and no. I think first you're going to want to speak with Dr. Vogel." He introduced me to the other man, the German. "Dr. Vogel is an oncologist."

"A *what?*" I know what an oncologist does; I was merely shocked to hear the word.

"Dr. Vogel specializes in radiation poisoning."

I stood up. "What does that have to do with anyth—?"

Dr. Vogel motioned me down. "Please, Miss Dunn. Sit."

I did.

Dr. Vogel asked me, "Miss Dunn, how did you pick the sample up from the ground?"

"By . . . by hand."

"I see. Did you carry it for long after that?"

"Actually, I did. It has a wonderful texture. It came from the sky. Just like that. Right in front of me. I dropped my groceries to go look at it."

"How long would you say, then?"

"I played with it for a few hours, and then . . ."

"And then what?"

"I've been sleeping with it beneath my pillow."

"I see."

"I think I do too."

More silence.

"How bad is it going to be for me, then?"

"I should think quite bad. I'm sorry."

* * *

Despite my wounding their economy, the Germans have treated me cheerfully. They also allowed me to be admitted to a real hospital, not just some slapdash prison infirmary.

The dirty bomb story was never allowed to make the newspapers (I suspect there are many stories like this that we never hear about), but the staff knew exactly who I was, what had transpired in the terminal—and also why I was now a guest in their hospital. I felt like an urban legend sprung to life: *You know, that crazy lady who thought this chunk of space junk was a meteorite. She stuck it in her luggage and shut down the world's seventh largest airport.*

I was placed in reverse isolation—yes, into the Bubble—as a precaution. I might have been immunosuppressed; others could easily pass their germs on to me. Dr. Vogel told me that the only real way to tell how severely one has been affected by radiation is by how rapidly the symptoms arrive. My blood tests hadn't yet come back, but if I were low on white blood cells, I'd be susceptible to opportunistic infections. I'm fortunate that immediate symptoms such as skin burns, nausea and fever hadn't occurred. I remember during Chernobyl seeing those poor doomed helicopter pilots pouring concrete over the melted reactor. They were dead within days. The thing is, Dr. Vogel doesn't know what, if anything, is going to happen to me. No one does. Symptoms could take months or years to occur, if ever.

Here I am in yet another form of isolation—a bubble, no less. What is the universe trying to tell me?

Dr. Vogel gave me an English-language medical book, but the section on radiation was too depressing. The symptoms are so similar to those of MS—all that's different are the rates at which they occur, and an overall sense of never quite knowing for sure if the end is really the end. Being in the Bubble only makes it worse. People look in and smile and wave at me as if I were a puppy or kitten—and the moment they pass, I bet they make a sad face at the person coming the other way: *Poor doomed woman in the Bubble.*

Near sunset, William walked into the room outside my bubble, his suit crinkled, a small tomato juice stain on his lapel. "Christ, Lizzie, what the fuck did you do to these people?"

"They didn't tell you?"

"Some, not all. You're in a fucking *bubble.*"

"Yes, I am."

"Are you sick?"

"Me? No."

"Why the bubble?"

"Technically, to protect me from you. They won't let me out until my white blood cell results come back. Pull up a chair."

William did so. "I drove down to your condo and the building was covered in white plastic. Guys with moon suits were going in and out, like at the end of *ET*. You're going to have some pretty pissed neighbours when you get home."

"That's occurred to me. You look tired."

"I haven't slept in twenty-eight hours. I'm used to it."

"Thank you for coming."

"So tell me what happened, okay?"

And so I did, leaving out the part about Herr Bayer and Klaus Kertesz.

William said, "That's our Lizzie—if you're not finding a transvestite sliced in two, it's a chunk of plutonium."

"Not plutonium—I believe it's enriched uranium."

He relaxed his chest and let out a whoosh of air. He

looked around. "You know what? I've bought blood from someone in this hospital before."

"That's a coincidence."

"Some of these Krauts chug along forever. This one woman remembered the invention of cars."

"Imagine having all those memories."

"She's got DNA like a dog's chew toy. She'll live to see World War Four."

"William, when you meet these people and you pay them for their blood, do you ever ask them anything?"

"Medical info only—smoking, drinking, diet—what their work was, how old their relatives are."

"Do they have anything in common?"

"They all say they don't worry very much—and weirdly, they tend to not like vegetables. It's true."

"I meant, do they ever say how they cope with having all those memories in their head?"

"Never. It's usually farmers, or people who live in small villages where nothing ever happens. People in cities never reach 105, let alone 110."

"Have you found anything yet that links them all together?"

"Maybe. We think there may be some gene markers, but the big money is going to be in, uh, *other* kinds of cells—but I'm not the one who told you that. We don't take just blood any more." He rubbed his eyes, winked and said, "I have to go sleep. How long are you here for?"

"If all goes well, I should be discharged in the morning. I have no clothes—my luggage is being buried as toxic waste—so I have to buy everything new."

He gave me the number of his hotel and we agreed to

meet after my release. As he was walking out of the room, he looked back at me in my bubble. "This is a bit like it was with Jeremy, isn't it?"

I said that it was.

He said, "See you in the morning, Lizzie."

* * *

I am determined to fly to Vienna quickly. As William doesn't know the real purpose of the trip, my determination to go leaves him confused. "Vienna? Just go home, Lizzie. You've had enough excitement already."

"No. I want to see Vienna." I was a free woman, my white blood cell count was fine and we were in the hotel's dining room, eating what can only be described as A Salute to Meat—veal stuffed with shrimp, pork stuffed with beef. But meat suddenly seemed different to me; it was flesh, perhaps radioactive flesh. The German word on the menu, *fleisch,* didn't help matters. I ended up eating a salad.

William was scheduled to fly home the next morning, and was giving me what he thought was good advice. "Vienna's a big old city filled almost exclusively with senior citizens. Trust me, I know old people, and that's all the city has—granted, not a 105 in the bunch. Is it the money you're worried about? Is your trip non-refundable?"

"It's not the money. I just want to go on principle." I was fiddling with my hair—or rather, the lack of it. That afternoon, before stocking up on my new *hausfrau* look, I'd impulsively gone into a salon and had it lopped off.

"And why on earth did you cut off your hair? It's your best feature."

"I'd rather do it myself than have chemo do it for me."

"Who said anything about chemo? Your white blood cell count was normal."

He was entirely correct, but it was easier to use chemo as an excuse instead of saying that I was really sick of being me and that I wanted to be someone else, if only for a little while. I think that's true of most people who radically cut their hair.

William finished the last veal on his plate. "Just make sure I'm there when Mother sees you for the first time. When are you off, then?"

"Tomorrow. I'm taking the train."

"Not flying?"

"No."

"The city of Frankfurt thanks you. Oh—I meant to ask you, do you get to keep your meteorite?"

"Of course not."

"It would make an interesting lawsuit if you tried to hold on to it."

"Be realistic, William. They'd simply have me shot."

We both stirred thick coffees. I was thinking over Dr. Vogel's prognosis for me. It wasn't bad, nor was it good. I'm slated to spend the rest of my life wondering whether a bit of fatigue is the start of something sinister, or if a bruise denotes underlying bad news.

I had asked the doctor, "You can't just do a blood test?"

"Miss Dunn, you could have one blood test a month for the rest of your life—maybe a white blood cell count, most likely—but then what would you do with the results?"

"You tell me."

"You'd just end up living in a state of hypochondria,

which I think is far worse for your body than most diseases out there."

"So I'm supposed to forget about it?"

"In a word, yes. And no."

I said good night and goodbye to William from the elevator. This is my journal up to now. I just swallowed a big German sleeping pill. Tomorrow: Vienna.

* * *

Once Jeremy's elevator started going down, it never came up again. It just fell and fell, into the centre of the earth, and then deeper some. After that first round of flu, he lost much of his mobility. A cold two months later stripped his face of much of its animation.

Sometimes I'd walk into the room and he'd be whispering to himself. I'd move in close to hear his words—always nouns, frightening in the way they formed into lists: . . . *black cotton* . . . *lemon groves* . . . *darkness* . . . *vinegar* . . . *broken bones* . . . *milk-white horses* . . . *nakedness*. When he stopped making his own jottings, I sometimes wrote down the words. I'd ask him about them, but when he was feeling more himself, he had no idea of their meaning.

I'm trying hard here not to overstate the boundaries of how well I came to know my son. Jeremy was damaged, complex and confused, and there's only so much one can learn about a person in a fixed amount of time. You can fake many things in life, but twenty years of history isn't one of them.

I have this theory about life and its shortness. I think that in order for us to take in everything there is for us to learn as human beings on this planet, we'd have to be alive for 750 years. Don't ask me how I came up with that number; it simply feels about right. As most of us only make it to 70, we're left with a deficit of 680 years' worth of experience. We can be empathetic, we can read every biography ever written, we can keep the TV locked onto the History Channel, we can swab the sores of lepers—but there always remain those annoying 680 years we'll never know about. I think that's why we believe in ideas bigger than ourselves: our short lifespan shortchanges us of knowledge of the profound.

I ran this by William one night while Jeremy was semi-asleep. He said, "Lizzie, you're pissed because you think you had a chance to know your kid but you blew it. Get over yourself. Look at me—I'll never really know my two brats. I know all the usual dad shit, but how far does that take me?"

Jeremy heard this. "Your kids are monsters. You don't discipline them—they're barn cats."

I said, "Jeremy!"

"Liz, my kids *are* monsters. I was one too. So were you."

"I've never thought of myself as a monster."

"Lizzie the burglar."

This took me aback. *"Burglar?"*

"We all knew about you breaking into houses."

Jeremy lifted his head for that one. "She *what?*"

My ears were burning.

"In the summers. Your mother went into houses when people weren't there, and she'd just sit around."

"Doing what?"

"Nothing. She just went into people's houses and sat in them."

I asked him, "How long have you *known* about this?"

"The police came around once when you weren't home. A woman from Social Services said it was just a phase, that we should ignore it. Mother took that advice very seriously."

Jeremy said, "Wait—the authorities allowed you to break and enter?"

In unison, William and I said, "It was the seventies. Things were different."

Jeremy looked at me. "So, Mom—did you steal *any*-thing?"

"No. That wasn't the reason." I confronted William. "Why did nobody ever tell me they knew?"

"My point exactly. There's much to be said for simply leaving your kids be."

Whatever they said next passed me right by. I was pink with embarrassment, and felt foolish for having thought I'd gotten away with something.

Wait—

Wait—

It was nothing—just a few of those European ambulances buzzing by outside the hotel window. Actually, my digs here in Vienna consist of a three-room suite—big and expensive, and I don't care. I just couldn't face the prospect of a single room, even a deluxe one. Not that I minded my night in prison and in the Bubble; I just don't want to be alone in one more single room this particular week.

The train floated from Frankfurt to Vienna, and the taxi ride from the station also couldn't have been more charming: chocolate- and cream-coloured pigeons, precisely coiffed grey hair, cement ornaments like cake frosting, and cookies on doilies looming around every corner. Vienna was never wrecked by war, so, like Rome, it's old and curlicued. Frankfurt was bombed to smithereens, so everything there is new and rectangular. Everything back home is new and rectangular, but only because it's the cheapest way of building; how nice to have had a curlicued patch somewhere out here in the world.

It's also odd to visit a city more by happenstance than by desire. Walking through Vienna's streets, I think, *Isn't that pretty. Oh my, look at that.* I see picturesque things, but nothing sticks to my brain, nor do I want things to. I'm detached.

Mostly I just looked in shop windows. Centuries of tweaking have rendered them irresistible, and even a cobbler's shop had a beautiful colourful display that made me pine for soles in need of releathering. After some hours I returned here to my suite. I was on my bed, holding my shoes, studying their heels, when my phone rang. It was Herr Bayer. I'd left a message on his machine. I'd forgotten to phone from the German hospital to announce my lateness; he must surely consider me a flake.

"Good afternoon, Miss Dunn."

"Herr Bayer, hello. I'm sorry I didn't call you before this. I was . . . *delayed*."

"I am honoured to have an international crime superstar on the phone with me in my humble office."

I played it dumb. "Oh?"

"I hear that the city of Frankfurt chased you out of town with stones and buckets of tar."

He found my story amusing, and my pride was pricked. "How did you find out?"

"This is Europe, Miss Dunn. We share information here.

I'm assuming you are okay after prison. What are you doing for dinner?"

"I hadn't thought about it."

"Then you must please join me."

We agreed to meet in the downstairs restaurant at eight o'clock, but I wondered if that was too early, too gauche—the Viennese probably start dinner at ten. Screw it. I looked at my short hair in the mirror. *What have I done? Well, long hair didn't take you far, Lizzie.* I realized I felt like I was primping for a date, and in so doing, alarm bells went off. *Liz Dunn has never been out on a date.* I knew almost nothing about Herr Bayer, and I suspected he was only out to cadge a dinner he could expense.

I rode down to the lobby in the elevator—a *Chitty Chitty Bang Bang* brass job that did everything but boil water and make tea. As I rode, I considered the conversation that was to come, and I felt somehow unarmed. Herr Bayer must surely have done his research on me. Did he know about Jeremy? He seemed like he'd know everything. I knew almost nothing. But we each had what the other needed, or that was my impression.

Down in the lobby, the hotel continued to be a dream. I remembered seven years back, watching daytime TV with Jeremy, and how, whenever somebody won a trip to France or someplace European, their hotel was always described as "sumptuous." This place *was* sumptuous. No surface was without lace, carved pearwood, bevelled mirrors, dark, oily paintings, thick fabrics, or whipped cream and a cherry. It was the opposite of my German jail cell. I felt alien, but when I caught a glimpse of myself in a mirror, I thought, *Oh, there's an Austrian person*—but then of course it was me being unfamiliar with my new short haircut and my new, non-radioactive outfit.

I felt like me, but not me. I suppose it's why we like travelling; it's why cults target airports, why train stations sell the flags of all nations. Travel dissolves you. It makes you need to rebuild yourself, forces you to remember where you're from.

"Miss Dunn?"

I turned around to see a man my age, average height, a beard and moustache, and slightly old-fashioned clothes. "Herr Bayer . . ."

We shook hands. "Please, the restaurant is this way, shall we go?"

He escorted me by the elbow, which nobody had ever done for me before. The gesture was corny yet reassuring. He reminded me of a cab driver I once met in Seattle, a bearded grump who said he was once Director of Theoretical Astrophysics at Kiev University.

The head waiter didn't look at me, but since I was escorted by a man, we didn't even break our pace and went directly to a table. By myself, I would have read the day's paper three times before being smuggled to the rearmost table.

We sat down.

"It is a pleasure finally to meet, Miss Dunn."

"Likewise." Heavy white napkins were unfurled on our laps. "It's nice to visit the city where the subconscious was invented."

He looked at me darkly. "Miss Dunn, the subconscious was not *invented*. It was *discovered*."

"Oh. Sorry. I hadn't given it much thought. I've always

thought we had our day-to-day personality and then we also have this big rat's nest inside of us called our subconscious."

"What makes you think of it as a rat's nest?"

"Well, if our subconscious was attractive, we wouldn't have to bury it down deep inside ourselves. It'd be just another feature on our face, like our nose." I could see Herr Bayer thought I might be joking, but I wasn't. "People talk about our subconscious like it's the South Pole and it required vast amounts of technology and determination to finally reach the place. How do we know there aren't five or six hidden layers of personality? Or sixty-two?"

"I think maybe four."

"What would you call them?"

"Miss Dunn, you already know that—your public self, your private self and your secret self."

"That's only three."

"The fourth is the dark self—the one that drives the car; the one that has the map; the one that is greedy or trusting or filled with hate. It's so strong it defies speaking."

Menus were given to us, and I snapped out of what felt like a trance. "How did we get here so quickly?"

"I think you were driving the car, Miss Dunn." He smiled, then ordered mineral water for us. A beautiful basket of bread appeared, with butter.

To compensate for such an off-kilter start, I prattled on about how beautiful Vienna was, and recounted, quite boringly, everything I'd seen that afternoon. In response he said, "You've a touch of sun on your face."

After my afternoon walk, my cheeks had the nice, slightly pulled-tight feel to them. "Oh. I suppose." I added, "But the sun is overrated, you know."

"Why is that, Miss Dunn?"

"Here you have this vast globe of flaring plasma that can be seen from trillions of light years away, and yet all it has circling it is a dozen or so rocks. You'd think something that cosmic would have a bit more going for it."

"Your way of looking at the universe is unique, Miss Dunn."

"I try to be realistic about things."

"The menu here is excellent."

"It's in German, Herr Bayer. Could you order for me?"

"Please, call me Rainer. And yes, I will. Are you allergic to anything?"

"No. But I have trouble with any meat whose name also describes what the meat used to do before it became meat."

"Such as . . ."

"Such as liver. Or kidney."

"Go on."

"*'Hi—before I was sautéed in onions, I spent my life refining impurities from a cow's bloodstream.'*"

"I see what you mean."

"I include sweetbreads and tripe on that list."

"What is a sweetbread?"

"A thymus gland."

"Tripe?"

"Stomach."

"Okay. Why don't we have Wiener schnitzel for dinner? When in Rome, do as the Romans do."

Romans. He'd quickly gotten to the point. "Rainer, you want to discuss our business right away?"

"No. No—I didn't intend for that coincidence. But the

fact that you came all this way on the basis of a few phone calls and a jpeg is tantalizing."

"I think I need to eat."

"Of course. And you must tell me about your German prison adventure."

"Where to begin?"

"Let's begin when you first found the piece of fuel from the Soviet satellite."

"Very well. It was a week ago Thursday—"

My story took us right through dinner, and I pride myself that it wasn't the least bit dull. I felt cosmopolitan. I thought that this must be how Leslie feels every day of her life, how beautiful people must go through existence, their every word a pastry for the starved. Rainer had also done his homework. He knew about William and his company, and he was able to help me decode the strange first six hours in Frankfurt during which there seemed to be no logic in what people were and weren't asking me.

We were near the end of our schnitzels when I realized we were running out of time to discuss Klaus Kertesz. Rainer saw this in my face and said, "It's perhaps better if we wait until tomorrow to discuss our official business, Miss Dunn."

"Liz." I was glad he felt this too. I was bagged.

"Liz. Come down to our police station and we can work more efficiently. Can you wait until then?"

"Of course."

The rest of the dinner was spent discussing Vienna. Throughout it all, Rainer was the perfect host, and not once did he make me feel I was torturing him with my presence.

Around eleven, we said good night in the lobby. I would come to the station the next morning at eleven.

Just before leaving, Rainer asked me, "Liz—do you ever buy lottery tickets?"

"What a strange question. Why, are you selling them?"

"No. I'm curious. Do you?"

"No, I don't."

"And why not?"

"Nobody's ever asked me that, but I have a definite opinion on the matter. Imagine, Rainer, if I'd bought a ticket and then had all of the numbers except for one. A failure that large I couldn't begin to imagine. Why open your door to that kind of grief, let alone pay money to have it happen to you?"

"There we have it. Good night, Liz."

"Good night, Rainer."

I am beyond pooped.

And, the hotel left cookies by my bedside.

Good night.

* * *

Rainer's office was drab in a generic bureaucratic way that even curlicued Vienna was powerless to change. It had nicotine-stained panelled walls in blue and grey and green. The office's cubicles were partitioned by filmy glass panes. The absence of fabric-panelled wall partitions and empty team-speak pep posters saved the precinct from resembling Landover Communication Systems. And cigarette smoke. Now that I think about it, it's not just the all-pervasiveness of cookies in Vienna that's weird, it's the pervasiveness of cigarettes. It's like seeing spittoons on every corner. What next—scarlet letters?

I also caused a small sensation when I entered Rainer's office, along the lines of, *Die Frau who upgefucked the entire Frankfurt Flugplatz vier days ago.*

"Liz, please. In here." Rainer motioned me in. On his desk was a coffee and, yes, another cookie.

"Rainer, what is it with Vienna and cookies?"

"What do you mean?"

"Everywhere I go here, people are giving me cookies. Is it something you people do to loosen the subconscious or something?"

"Liz, a small amount of sugar is surely good for the release of ideas and memories."

"So it's a plot, then."

"A plot?"

I could see that staff members were pretending not to gawk at me from outside the windows.

"Ignore my colleagues," said Rainer. "You are a celebrity. We do not see them often." From a desk drawer he pulled a cheap, legal-seeming black vinyl photo album, but he appeared reluctant to open it.

"Is that for me to look at?" I asked.

"Yes. But not yet." He lit a cigarette and said, "Liz, last night was social, and a very enjoyable evening, but we chose not to probe into the matter of Rome, and of Herr Kertesz."

"That was polite of you. Thank you. Yes, it was a nice evening."

"Liz, you flew here to meet with me. I can only infer some deep connection between you and Herr Kertesz."

"Klaus Kertesz? Yes."

"Can I ask you now—my office is soundproof—to tell me what I need to know about this man—as regards *you?*"

What was I to say? This was the moment he'd been waiting for. My arms clenched across my chest, protecting my rib cage. I spotted sky-blue background on the edge of the photo poking out from the vinyl album—the same blue that was on the jpeg of Klaus Kertesz that had started this whole odyssey.

That sliver of blue was all I needed. I began huffing and puffing, quite against my will, an anxiety attack, my first, and I was no better than Scarlet Halley, five miles over Reykjavik. It occurs to me that, like Scarlet on the 747, and like Jeremy on my condo's sofa, I'd finally found a place in which I felt secure enough to disintegrate—across from this stubbly Eurocratic man who looked like Václav Havel's cellmate. Next, I began to blubber in the large, messy way I tried to avoid my entire life. I can think of nothing more repelling than *me,* in tears, making a scene *in public,* demanding attention, even if that was never the purpose of my tears.

After I calmed down, Rainer passed me my cookie and topped up my coffee. "I assumed there was something there. Perhaps you could tell me what happened."

Boosted by mind-opening sucrose, I told Rainer about Rome, and about Jeremy, and I took almost an hour to do so. Upon finishing, I was wiped out, and Rainer said, "Why don't I take you to lunch."

So we walked to a bistro, and he kept the discussion light, which at that moment suited me well. Vienna is a stunning city, a tourist's dream, but in their numbers the tourists diminished the city's charm. What would the pious citizens of other centuries have made of the thousands of sweaty, near-naked tourists now buzzing like mites in and out of their cathedrals?

Once we were inside the bistro, Rainer's mood changed. He said, "Maybe it would have been better if Vienna had been bombed in the war. Everything here is so monstrously old. Sometimes I'm jealous of the Germans—at least *they* were able to create something new." He paused. "Sorry. What an awful thing to say. But I would very much like to see a UFO land and take half the city with it. Maybe the Chinese will do it someday." He scanned a menu that he must have seen thousands of times during his career. "We happened to be big and middle-class first. All these people with not enough trouble in their lives creating new ways to create trouble." He looked out the front window. "Let us eat."

We ordered lunch—onion soup with Gruyère, salad and steak, pommes frites—and, shortly after, it arrived.

"So," asked Rainer, "what shall we do about Herr Kertesz?"

"Well, I think I'd like to meet him."

"I haven't told you much about him."

"Even so."

He ate, said nothing, but I stopped eating and stared at him, and won the match. He said, "I suppose I cannot stop you."

"No, you can't. Tell me about him."

"Very well."

"Is he in jail?"

"No."

"Is he a criminal?"

"Not technically. Some petty theft when he was young, but nothing after twenty. If a man steals at twenty-five, he will steal at fifty. So, he is not a criminal. Not that way."

"How else, then?"

Rainer poured us both some water. "He is what you would call a public nuisance. He is annoying, but technically, legally, he's doing nothing wrong."

"What kinds of things?"

"He talks to himself on the street."

"*I've* been known to do that. On the phone you said assaults against women. That sounds pretty serious to me. What kind of assaults?"

"Not sexual assaults."

This wasn't what I was expecting to hear. "What? Okay—then what kind?"

Rainer didn't want to say what he said next, but he finally got it out. "Religious assaults."

"What?"

"It has nothing to do with suggestive clothing or that strain of zealotry. Herr Kertesz selects women—though we have no idea how he selects them—and he decides that they need a . . . religious education."

"Is this some kind of Catholic Austrian thing?"

"No. His family is Protestant, but he seems non-denominational."

"Is he trying to be Charles Manson?"

"No."

"Is he poor, and scamming for money?"

"Quite the opposite. Herr Kertesz's family takes good care of him. He is also a dentist and successful."

"What does he do to the women he—confronts?"

"He follows them around, and he asks them questions."

"Like . . . ?"

He made a face to tell me that he'd memorized Klaus Kertesz's pickup lines. "Like, *Your life is too easy. You've been tricked into not questioning your soul. Do you know this?*"

"And . . . ?"

"*Unless you change quickly, your soul will freeze itself into one shape forever, and never thaw. You must know this. Have you thought about it?*"

"He sounds tame enough."

"Liz—imagine you're just an ordinary woman trying to go from the office to the market to the house, having to deal with this—" He refrained from saying "idiot," but I could tell that Klaus Kertesz was blighting Rainer's days.

"He's a stalker, then."

"No. A stalker stalks. Herr Kertesz keeps to his own routine, but if he bumps into one of the women on his list, he acts."

"Is there any sort of ongoing type of woman he annoys?"

"They tend to be his own age, and also, women at first do not mind, as he's tall and very good-looking."

"Has he ever hassled men?"

"No. We've questioned him several times. He says that men are all damned, and that there is no use trying to save them. He says only women can be saved, and that's why there are slightly more women born than men—so that we, as humans, have hope. He's statistical about it."

I asked, "But he's never actually assaulted a woman?" *What about me?*

"No. He's a nuisance, but not an attacker. Or so we

thought. But a month before I found you on Google, there was a woman here who became tired of Mr. Kertesz's attentions. One night as she was walking home, Mr. Kertesz zoomed in to deliver his lecture. She performed some tae kwon do moves on him, and after this she filed a formal assault charge. This pleased me. We were glad because we finally had legal recourse. It was after our interview with him that he told us about you. I did not expect you to actually come here."

"That was almost three decades ago. What could I possibly say or do now that would make any legal difference—or *any* difference?"

"Maybe nothing."

"But here I am, right now, sitting in front of you."

"Yes."

"Rainer, I guess we could have had this small conversation on the phone."

"Technically."

"I need to think a minute."

It was a relief to find out that Klaus wasn't a rapist, but again, what happened to *me?* It was obvious Bayer wanted to give Kertesz enough rope to hang himself with, and if it got a rapist off the street, good. But how to digest the news that he was a religious—what? A religious . . . *streetwalker?* "Do any of these women ever stop and actually talk to him?"

"As I said, he's a handsome man, and he shows interest."

"But then what happens?"

"I think the women realize that they're not being treated as individual women, but only as a part of Herr Kertesz's sickness. Something about his banter—is that the word?—something about his banter makes them suspicious."

"How can you know that?"

"When you meet him, you'll see for yourself."

What I expected to see was an older version of Jeremy, one who wasn't sent to multiple rural British Columbian foster homes, who didn't get MS and who didn't have to put a brave face on the crappy hand life had dealt him. I said, "When we go back to your office, can you show me more of the photos you have of Klaus?"

"No, I can show them to you right now."

From his leather attaché case he removed the vinyl photo album. He moved our mineral water glasses so that I could lay it flat on the table. I saw, laid out, maybe a dozen photos that showed Klaus over the past decade, aging well, the only noticeable change being the deepening creases in his brow and the creases running from the sides of his nose down to his jaw.

"Does he resemble your Jeremy?"

"Yes. He does. Almost entirely."

"How do the photos make you feel?"

For the first time in my life I had the sensation that I was being analyzed, that something alien was tracking and monitoring my statements and behaviour, and assessing them on a scoresheet in categories I couldn't imagine. How fitting that it be in Vienna.

"How does it make me *feel?* It makes me feel stupid, for not remembering this Kertesz guy in the first place. It makes me sad, because I miss Jeremy so goddamn much. But most of all—you know what?—it makes me hopeful, because now I can see where Jeremy really came from."

"You'd still like to meet with Herr Kertesz, then?"

"More than ever."

"You're not afraid?"

"Me? No."

"Perhaps not about physical assault, but about being . . ."

"Being what?"

Rainer shrugged. "Let down, perhaps?"

"How?"

"That maybe Herr Kertesz somehow makes smaller your memory of Jeremy."

"No. I can't believe that. Not until I meet the man." Though I confess I was feeling as though I'd just released the genie from the bottle.

Rainer said to me, "And so you shall meet him."

I said, "Good."

At that moment the room flashed white and I almost passed out, hit suddenly with a blinding headache. After the headache's first assault, I emerged into reality, dazed. Rainer was asking if I was okay. I looked in the mirror behind him and saw that I was chalk white. I'd never seen a body do that before, let alone mine.

"Liz, I'll take you back to your hotel right now."

"It's nothing."

"No, it's probably MSG in the lunch."

"You're probably right." But of course with me, after Frankfurt, a headache is no longer *just* a headache.

He taxied with me back to my hotel, where I slept until sunrise the next morning—today—this morning.

I'm scheduled to meet Klaus Kertesz at three this afternoon, in a room at the City Hall. I can only say that I'm glad to have had my pen and paper to chip away at the time between then and . . . thirty minutes from now.

Time to go.

* * *

In the cab to City Hall, my head felt like an oven that had been burning full tilt all day long, with no food inside being cooked. I was a mess.

Rainer met me at the front door and escorted me inside, where it was cool, across marble floors buffed by centuries of genteel shoe leather. We walked quickly to a room at the end of a long second-floor hallway. We stopped at a wooden door. The upper half was a rippled-glass window through which I could see a figure inside.

Rainer asked me, "You're okay here?"

"Does he know it's me?"

"No."

"How did you convince him to come?"

"It was more his family. They want the noise around him to go away."

I said I was ready, and I entered the room.

There, more or less, was Jeremy, but much older. He'd been looking out the window, and when he turned around to see me, he gave me Jeremy's winning smile.

Klaus took one step toward me and said, "Well, good heavens. Queen Elizabeth. Hello."

* * *

Just so it doesn't look like I'm building toward a fireworks climax here, I'll flatly say that Jeremy died on the morning of December 23—after just four months of living with me. I was in the bathroom counting his pills, and when I came out I found that his body had just sort of . . . stopped. His last words were a small joke, about an hour earlier: *This mattress is both comfortable and affordably priced.*

There. I feel better having gotten that out of the way. His death came far more quickly than anyone had anticipated, but MS is a crapshoot.

Just so nobody forgets, here's a list of some of Jeremy's symptoms:

numbness
pins and needles
blurred vision
inability to walk
inability to tolerate heat
muscle spasms
swallowing problems
loss of sensation
loss of bladder and bowel control
dementia

Most people with MS have a plausibly normal life and can manage through the years okay. Jeremy was "primary progressive." Primary progressives take a gut-kneading high-speed ride that can't, won't and is unable to stop once it begins. His final diet was mostly pills and IVs: prednisone, Betaseron and glatiramer acetate. Mostly the meds made him nauseous or confused, but every so often they triggered a good evening's conversation. On the plus side, Jeremy never had mood swings or bouts of apathy, common in the late stages of MS. I was grateful for that. His humour and charm never once vanished.

It was those damned nodules of dead proteins in his brain, like raisins in raisin bread, that stripped Jeremy of the motions and tics and gestures that make us alive. I have to remind myself of the medical view, because I could see no message from God there—no mercy, no higher logic or moral sense to describe the sight of him on my couch, as fall merged into winter, as Hale-Bopp came and went, and as, near the end of November, he finally lost his winning smile.

I was giving him a haircut one afternoon. He looked at me and said, "Mom, come on, it has to be showing. I'm trying here."

"Sorry, honey."

"Crap. That smile was going to coast me right through my golden years."

By December, Jeremy had lost so many of his Jeremy-isms that the loss of the winning smile seemed, to him, anticlimactic. To me it was hard, as it was his winning smile that had carried me over to his side of the universe. Remember, this is a man who had me crawling down a highway in rush hour on the first day we met.

Dr. Tyson came every few days, powerless to do much except watch and prescribe more pills. She went beyond the call of duty and taught me about practical issues like drips, tubes and wheelchairs. I pride myself that I was competent in that respect.

William was good for a visit every few days, and when he came he brought snippets gleaned from the medical underground—yes, a medical underground exists—and these snippets provided us with dim glimmers of hope. It's amazing how far you can go along bartering with a disease. *If we could just fly to Baltimore to try this new antibody therapy, all our problems would be solved!* Denial was easy; bargaining was the toughie. Stem cells now offer genuine hope, but as recently as seven years ago—zip. Mother and Leslie did their part too, which was simply to visit.

I also kept on hand the best medicine of all: volumes of literature on farming, which Jeremy enjoyed reading or having read to him. When he was too prostrate to do anything much, I read aloud the dos and don'ts of allowing alfalfa fields to go fallow, the proper procedures for piglets who won't suckle, or the advantages of renting a light plane and viewing your land from above. Along the windows we had a small farm of runner beans and radishes growing in a variety of Styrofoam containers. If I ever go on a quiz show and the topic is farming, just watch me win that minivan with the built-in Warner Brothers TV package.

* * *

Okay, I see what I'm doing here—I'm using medicine and science to deflect attention away from what it was that made my son himself and different in a big way: his visions—his, oh *God*—I don't care what you call them at this point. Whatever it was, Jeremy *saw* something uncanny. Period.

One afternoon I was reading a magazine and he said, "Can you see them?"

I said, "What?"

"The air in front of us. It's filled with metal tubes."

"Tubes?"

"Like for road drainage. They're floating around in front of us—and now they're entering my body. I have holes going through my body. Tunnels." He was looking at the ceiling as he said this.

I wrote down his words as he spoke. "What else do you see?"

"I'm looking down at the ground, but I'm not casting a shadow. Instead of my shadow there's light."

"And?"

"I've walked into a dark room. There's a planet in front of me now. Earth. It's maybe your height. It's glowing like the old NASA footage—in the middle of the room. Floating."

"What's it doing?"

"Nothing. Hovering. If I went up to it and blew, I could cause a hurricane anywhere I wanted. I just touched Antarctica. It's cold. And now I'm looking at my fingers."

"Go on."

"The earth is so bright. My hands are glowing bright red from the blood inside them."

"Okay."

Jeremy went quiet for awhile.

"Anything else?" I asked.

"No. Nothing."

"Keep trying."

After a few seconds he said, "I'm never going to know you properly, Mom. You know that."

"I do."

"I should have contacted you years earlier."

"Nonsense."

"I'm not going to be seeing any more pictures in my head." I was about to protest, but he said, "Mom, *no*. It's over. You're the one who has to do it now."

"I can't."

"No. If I can inherit something as stupid as being able to sing backwards from you, you can certainly see a few pictures in your head."

It was late afternoon, a weekday, and I breathed in a few times and closed my eyes, at which point Jeremy said, "Try to find the farmers."

And so I tried.

What do any of us see when we close our eyes? Nothing and everything. I've often wondered what sort of dreams people have who are born blind. Do they dream in sound and temperature? Has anybody ever documented this?

For obvious reasons, I've thought about "seeing things" a great deal since then. For starters, I think humans are the only animal to know the difference between sleeping and dreaming. It doesn't matter if you're a lion cub, a jellyfish or a fern—wakefulness and dreaming are the same thing to them all. I think that until recently, maybe a few thousand years ago, that was the case for humans too. But then there was somebody out there who broke the cycle, who told people the difference between the two worlds. And so, for a few centuries, people became used to thinking of real life and dreaming as two different places. And it was someone like Jeremy who did the telling.

But then something else happened. While we knew about dream life versus real life, we still didn't know about the past, present or future. A day was a day was a day.

tomorrow = yesterday = today = the same thing = always

There had to be somebody out there who made a radical leap—someone who told the others that there existed this place beyond us that was different than anything we'd known, namely the future. And because of the future, all human lives became different. Our children's lives became different, *better* than ours. We could apply our minds to being more efficient in the way we did tasks. And it was someone like Jeremy who told people this.

And then someone came along and told people that on top of everything else, not only was there life and death, but there was also life *after* death. And it was someone like Jeremy who told people this. Jeremy's job was to be a teller, and now he'd decided to pass that job on to me.

Back in the living room that afternoon, I said I would apply myself to trying to see the farmers, with little hope of success.

* * *

Klaus Kertesz said, "You remember me, don't you, Elizabeth?"

"No, I don't." It took everything out of me just to play it cool. Remember, I have no memory of Jeremy's conception. *Was* this guy a rapist? *Was* I complicit in my own pregnancy? I couldn't allow myself to be judgmental. The final fact of the matter was that he *did* give me Jeremy. Ends don't justify the means, but I, Liz Dunn, once had a child. And I, Liz Dunn, also knew that if I wanted to hear the truth about my night in Rome, I would have to maintain a calm exterior. Accusations and tears would get me nothing, and I'm sick of nothing.

Klaus is also, as Rainer told me, almost stupidly handsome, and it's difficult to speak with beautiful people. No matter how hard you try to pretend otherwise, you still want them to like you. We are a wretched, shallow species.

Klaus shook my hand, and as he did I briefly crumbled at the knees. We wait so long for moments like this in life, and when they finally occur, we blunder through them the same way we do everything else. Me? The last person on earth to be paralyzed by looks, but there I go. Stupid, *stupid* Lizzie.

He said, "You don't remember me. I can see that. How sad. I remember you so well."

That anyone ever remembers me at all is invariably a surprise, but to be remembered well? "*Do* you?"

"Of course. That trip to Rome. It was all of our parents sending us away so that they could go to Scandinavia without children. Our trip had no educational value. It was, how do you say, a piss-up. Did you enjoy Rome?"

"Yes."

"But you don't remember me?"

"No."

Klaus looked at Rainer. "Herr Bayer, I'm sure you're the one who found Elizabeth."

"You are correct."

"But even having found Elizabeth, why on earth *would* you locate her? She is a . . ."—he looked my way—" . . . happy evening from my very distant past."

"It is my job to follow up on all possible leads."

"Leads? Leads to what?" Klaus turned to me. "Elizabeth, why did you come all the way to Vienna from Canada—you still live there, yes?"

"Yes."

"Why would you come all this way to meet somebody you don't remember? You both confuse me."

It felt premature to mention Jeremy. I was stuck for words. I didn't know if I wanted to kill this man or lick his neck and stick my tongue in his ear.

He seemed truly distraught that I didn't remember him. He asked me, "What has Mr. Bayer told you about me that was so inviting?"

I said, "Not much. That you make religious . . . *assaults* on women. That's probably the wrong phrase. But you must know what I'm speaking about."

"Oh yes, but you see, I no longer do that any more."

Rainer cut in here. "What do you mean, you no longer do?"

"I've been given medicines. Paroxetine. I started to take it three weeks ago, and it's already turned off the part of my brain that needs to do that."

Rainer was dubious. "That's bullshit, Herr Kertesz."

"If you want to believe that, then please do. But I passed two of my previous, uh, friends this morning, and I had no desire to talk with them. I have been diagnosed as an obsessive-compulsive, and that is a condition that, in 2004, is now quite controllable. Fifteen years of Freudian therapy, an adulthood wasted, for nothing. Suddenly I take this little pill and *voilà!* I am normal, just like everybody else. Tell me, Elizabeth, do you have friends who leave their houses then panic and run back inside to see that the stove is switched off?"

"Yes. Jennifer from Human Resources. She'll go back to the cafeteria kitchen four or five times until she's calm. She once wrote the word *Off* on her forearm."

"Exactly. The way medicine is being designed now, I'm sure they'll have a drug called Stovex that will act specifically on people with stove compulsions."

"You're probably right."

"Thank you. Now could you please tell me the real reason you came?"

Rainer nodded at me. I reached into my purse and pulled out a pile of snapshots of Jeremy—dozens that I had taken (winning smile included) as well as the two sad little pictures from his social worker. I laid them out on the table in a long row. Most were at the condo, but some were at the beach, and one was taken at the top of Grouse Mountain on the clearest of days, the city behind him glinting like a summer lake. As Klaus's eyes hit the first shot, I felt it was compassionate to say, "I'm sorry to tell you he's dead, Klaus. About seven years ago."

Zealot or not, what a horrible dose of good news/bad news to get at once. He sat down at the table, holding a few of the shots, and I wondered if I'd done the right thing in coming.

"What was his name?"

"Jeremy."

"What type of man was he?"

"He was a nice guy. I only met him four months before he died. He was adopted at birth. I never knew him until he found me."

"How did he die?"

"Multiple sclerosis." I looked in my purse. "I brought a VHS tape here with me, but it won't work on European machines."

Rainer said, "We can take it down to the station. Our system can handle your format."

I sat down opposite Klaus, as did Rainer. Out of respect, we let him look at the photos without us scrutinizing him.

Rainer asked how my head felt. I said, "It's actually much better. I think it's the jet lag and everything else catching up with me."

"Of course it is." Rainer was a bit too quick with the *of course.*

"Thank you for the codeine pills."

"I have many more if you like. My job."

Klaus looked up and said, "Please, let's go to the police station."

We drove to the station in Rainer's car, with me up front, Klaus in the back, silent and grimacing out the window. There were clouds of pigeons, flocks of Japanese tourists, and masonry so ornate and delicate that it seemed to be dreaming.

At the station, we passed through several elevators and corridors and ended up in a room with a VCR. Klaus sat down while Rainer showed me how to use the machine.

I said, "This is from my birthday party in November 1997, at my mother's house. Jeremy still had some control of his facial muscles then. We were all a little bit drunk. He died about a month after this. It was the last night that everything worked all together at once."

"Please, let me see it."

I turned it on, and as always I was surprised the tape hadn't eroded since then. There was some crackling and a squeal and then the sound of me, Jeremy, Mother, William and William's two brats, but not Nancy, who that evening had decided to sulk at the far end of the room. Leslie and her family were hiking on Vancouver Island.

I was the evening's cameraman. I started filming with William saying, "Come on, Jeremy, we need to give you a *man's* challenge."

"I can take whatever you can throw at me, you great spinner of lies."

My mother and I hooted, and the kids squeaked.

"Okay," said William, "try *this* . . ." William inserted a tape into the deck, a Japanese model with backward and forward motion. He turned it on, and on came "The Devil Went Down to Georgia," lightning-fast words, *Fire on the mountain, run boys run/ The devil's in the house of the rising sun . . .*

Jeremy shouted, "You insult me! Turn off the machine and let me sing my song!"

William fiddled with switches, and Jeremy promptly sang it backwards. Everybody turned to William. He replayed the tape—Jeremy had nailed it. It was a fun evening.

Klaus asked, "What were you *doing?*"

I paused the tape. "Singing songs backwards. It's a weird talent Jeremy inherited from me."

I turned the tape back on. William was saying, "Okay, buster, there's no stopping you. Why don't we have a crowd-pleaser?" William turned to the camera (me) and said, "Are we ready to rock!"

The two kids said, "Dad, shut up."

William said, "Are we ready to *rock!*"

"Dad, shut up. You're being a goof."

"Ladies and gentlemen, the crowd pleaser of all time: 'Bohemian Rhapsody'!"

. . . I see a little silhouetto of a man . . .

Jeremy said, "Man, I cut my teeth on this song. Sir William—hit your recording button!"

Jeremy stood up, a surprise in itself, and with full body control mimicked a Three Tenor. We were so floored by his performance that, when he was done, we went mute.

"Well?" said Jeremy. "A playback if you will?"

The playback was moot. We knew it'd be perfect, and it was.

I said, "Jeremy, is there anything you'd like to say to posterity?"

One of the kids asked, "What's posterity?"

Mother said, "Posterity is whether or not people remember you, dear."

Jeremy looked at the camera and slowly blew a kiss to the lens. "Hello posterity. Lovely to meet you at last." It was a pretty moment, like when a gust of plum blossoms hits your windshield in April. "Glad you could make it to our party."

"Speech!" Mother was lost to cognac.

"To posterity, and to everyone here in the room, I wish you peace, and prosperity, and a long and fine life." He blew another kiss at the camera. "See you later. Be nice."

The room remained quiet after that. Nancy, pragmatic as always, broke the uneasy silence, saying, "Let's just cut the goddamn cake." The two boys fought over who got to light the candles. The moment was over.

I turned off the VCR. "There's more. We had a karaoke marathon. William's kids can sort of sing backwards. William can't do it at all."

Rainer said, "I'll make you a copy of this tape later."

Klaus was rocking gently. Rainer left, and I sat down beside Klaus on a swivelling office chair. "Rainer never said if you had children. Do you?"

He was defeated. "No."

"Have you ever been married?"

"Me? No. I wish, but my compulsions always frightened the young gazelles."

There was a silence, and he asked if he could watch the tape alone. I left him there.

* * *

A few years ago, I started eating lunch at the hospital cafeteria every now and then. The food was passable, and my aim was to people-watch, trying to figure out what interior dramas preoccupied my fellow diners. This activity helped make my otherwise drama-free life three-point-seven percent more interesting. I mention this because, a half-hour later, Klaus emerged from the room with the TV set and, as he did, he reminded me of people in hospital lobbies—the disbelieving posture, the obviously churning soul, the stare that comes from helplessness. Rainer called him into his office to join us.

By then Klaus had connected all the dots, and understood why I'd come to Austria. He said, "You think I raped you, don't you?"

"I—really have no idea."

"You don't remember what happened?"

"No." There was another silence. I said, "Please. Tell me."

He said, "I doubt it's what you think. We went up onto the roof of that horrible discotheque—there was a group of us—eight maybe? We were all a little bit drunk, but you were far drunker than us."

"I remember that part."

"My friends were being stupid teenagers. They were spitting and throwing firecrackers down on the street. I probably would have joined them, but you were drunker than I thought. I was worried about you. My friends were all saying, 'Sissy! Nursie-poo!' That kind of thing. They wanted to go downstairs and pick up your girlfriends, and so they left us. I was trying to think of a way of taking you downstairs, but that was hard. The roof wasn't flat—it was covered with pipes and metal boxes and wires. And you were quite . . ."

"I'm a large woman, Klaus. It's a fact."

"Yes, well—I asked you about yourself. You said you were from Vancouver, and that you were the loneliest girl in the world. You said you were so tired of being lonely. You said that your favourite thing was to enter the houses of strangers and sit there and do nothing—just sit in their houses. I thought that was the saddest thing I'd ever heard."

I bit my upper lip.

"You were kind of crazy, and it was this side of you I don't think people see very often. Do you drink?"

Rainer raised an eyebrow at this question, but I knew what Klaus was driving at. "No, I don't. Because you know exactly what happens to me if I do."

"Okay. So you were being somewhat wild, and you asked me to kiss you, so I did. You said it was your first kiss ever, and I felt happy that I could be such a nice memory for someone. But then you wanted to go beyond kissing, and we were on the roof, and the Colosseum was right there, and we were in Rome, and—we did what we did. It was nice. I think you had a good time. It wasn't my first time, but I wish it was. It was romantic. I'm sorry you don't remember it."

"So am I."

There was nothing more to say on the matter. It was case closed, both for me and for Rainer. Of all things, I yawned, breaking the silence. I apologized to the men. "Sorry, it's not you. It's fallout from that godawful airport in Frankfurt."

Klaus asked, "You were caught in that too?"

"You might say so."

It turned out Klaus was one of the two million or so people who were inconvenienced when Frankfurt's airport discovered the space junk in my suitcase. He'd been waiting to pick up his mother, who was routing through Frankfurt on her way back from a botanical expedition in Iceland—lichens and moss. Klaus had driven back to the airport three times before her flight came in.

He looked at my face and Rainer's, and knew something larger had happened than merely being stuck at an airport. So we told him about the meteorite and everything that followed. Klaus was horrified. He's a dentist—he knows about alpha, beta and gamma rays. "The radiation—it could have been toxic. What numbers did they give you? What sort of documentation?"

"None."

"That's not possible. They must have given you something."

"I'm afraid not."

Klaus looked at Rainer. "This is astonishing. Who can I call to locate numbers on this?"

Rainer agreed, and the two men then went through indexes and computer files and compiled a list of names and numbers. As they did, I went into a happy trance, knowing that there wasn't just crap parked away in my subconscious, but also a big and happy memory somewhere too.

When the men had what they needed, they had to snap me out of my trance. "Yes—hello—"

Rainer said, "I'll drive you back to your hotel, Liz."

I suddenly went into a panic. I was going to be alone and lonely in a suite of rooms in a foreign city. My Viennese mission had been accomplished, and I was merely me again, no other mysteries hidden within, and with nothing but my condo and Landover Communication Systems awaiting my return.

Klaus said, "Let me take you to dinner tonight, Liz. It would make me happy."

I said yes, and the panic stopped.

* * *

When I came out of the bathroom and found Jeremy dead, I sat on a chair beside the bed that I'd bought him the month before. I held his hand, looked at his face and made a squeaking noise. I thought to myself, *Imagine that—somebody is making a squeaking noise.* Outside the window lay a boring, overcast mid-morning—a Tuesday. I heard the sounds of other people's lives continuing as always, and I felt as if I were from another galaxy. I thought of bodies, and I remembered Father's memorial service. He'd been cremated, so there'd been no body to contemplate. His ashes arrived from Honolulu in a courier's box, and that seemed so unfair, not to see the body first. I remembered how I once enjoyed looking at dead bodies on TV. No more of that for me.

I knew I had to phone somebody, but who? William, Nancy and the kids were in Disneyland. Leslie and her family were in Disney World. Mother wasn't in when I called, so in the end I phoned Dr. Tyson, and she arranged for the bureaucratic things—taking Jeremy away, and the paperwork.

On hanging up, I went to sit beside Jeremy again. I have to say that I felt like a space alien in a little UFO hovering about a foot over the shoulder of this woman called Liz. I sat for about an hour, looking at Jeremy amid his still life of empty pill bottles, uneaten plastic tubs of rocky road pudding, a stack of *Modern Farmer* magazines, piles of blankets, two bedpans, a TV remote control, a feeding machine—and then the ambulance arrived and took him away. Once he was gone, the sensation of detachment fled. I was fully me again, and I looked around my condo at The World's Emptiest Room and I knew I had to escape. I grabbed a white plastic shopping bag and stuffed it with a few bathroom things, a dress and some shirts, and drove to Mother's. She was returning from grocery shopping. As I pulled in, she knew what was up.

Mother's way of coping with things is to find some sort of medium-sized task and then hang on to it for dear life, which in this case was Jeremy's funeral service. It helped her through Father's death, and would allow her to cope with this too. The rest of the family wasn't slated to return from their Sunbelt pleasure domes until after Christmas. Mother, on the phone, was a lioness: "Your nephew, my grandson, is not going to sit in a deep-freeze just so you and Leslie can stand in line for Magic Mountain or Tinkerbell's frigging Jacuzzi. *They* can stay, but *you,* William, you, Leslie, are coming home for this. And yes, your sister will pay." In the end, Leslie and William returned for the service, on December 27.

Mother arranged the funeral and for the obituary notice

in the *Vancouver Sun*. We both wondered whom this notice might flush out—possibly some of Jeremy's people from his earlier lives, some foster family members. We would have called Kayla from Social Services, but they were closed.

Mother bought a casket that was like some sort of dying pimp's final wish: a metal-flaked maroon job with oak mouldings, chrome grilles, leather trim and a hood ornament. It was a kind gesture, if an odd one. "At your birthday party last month I was drinking red wine, and he said what a pretty colour it made with the kitchen lights shining through it. So I wanted to find one in that colour. I think it's quite close." And it was.

Christmas didn't happen that year. No point. On Boxing Day, I was thawing a little and getting a better grasp on things. Nonetheless, the thought of my condo made my head go black. Mother had to go in and fetch my things, which irked her. We were approaching the condo in Mother's car when she entered her sermon mode: "You know, Elizabeth, there's much to be said for simply hanging in there. Being in your own place will make you feel slightly normal again."

"I don't want to feel normal. And my place gives me the creeps. Don't even park on the same street."

"You're being melodramatic."

Mother turned left onto my street, and the sight of my building made my stomach clench.

"Elizabeth, come up and help me get your things."

"No."

"As usual, I'll have to be the one to get things done."

"Okay, Mother, you do that." I stayed in the car and

glared into the rhododendron shrubs across the street, where a marmalade cat was slinking toward unknown prey.

My apartment reminded me of everything I didn't want my life to be. I thought back to the time when I had a twin bed, not a queen or king. What sort of message would that have sent out to anybody, should I ever have brought anybody home?

I was sitting there thinking of this advice from my dead son when Mother rapped on the window. "I'm going to return your place to normal."

"What?"

"Somebody has to do it."

"Why now?"

"Because it's something to do, and if I leave it to you, it won't happen."

"I don't care."

Mother was trying hard not to lose it. "I'm going to be here for several hours, so either sit in the car or do what you will."

She burned back into the building. I stepped out of the car, walked down the block and took a bus to Mother's.

It doesn't take brains to infer that my fear of my apartment was, in reality, a fear of being lonely again. I'd entirely forgotten about loneliness until Jeremy's body was removed. I'd forgotten the thing I detest more than anything, the bile taste in my throat when I realize that it's nearing dinner and I have no evening plans. I'd also forgotten waking up on Saturday morning and realizing that I have two days to kill until work begins—the cold little chink of light between the curtain and the window frame that tells me I have no life. No matter how hard I tried coping—or how well I sometimes seemed to be doing—loneliness was still the dominant mood that tinted and diminished everything.

And I was aging.

I suspect that all human beings have a point where they realize that what they have is the most they're ever going to have, be it love, money or power. You have to make peace with who you are, and what you've become. I'd thought that a decision to choose peace instead of predictability was a simple bookkeeping decision that would easily reconcile me with my life. That was foolish. What it took was a taste of life on the other side of the mirror, with Jeremy, caring and being cared for. During his illness I told myself that his death was still a long way away, so loneliness wasn't something I had to deal with. What was I thinking? What sort of sicko person would find hope in the suffering of somebody else? Was I no better than Donna?

As I walked to the bus stop, I felt weak and sick, missing Jeremy and dreading the prospect of three more decades alone here on earth. I wanted the bus doors to open and the bus to fall down a deep hole in the earth where it would pancake into oblivion.

When I got back to Mother's, all I felt was relief that I was in a place where there would now be two people living, not one. How had she managed all these years on her own? She never seemed to care one way or the other. I mulled this over and felt even worse. But no—with Mother, what you see is all there is.

She walked in the door around seven, saying, "All done."

"How 'all' do you mean?"

"Everything. I even had your landlord move the bed down into the storage locker along with Jeremy's things. I stuck anything medical in a U-Haul box and dropped it off at the hospital. To walk in, you'd never know there'd been another person in there all this time but you."

* * *

"That must have felt awful."

"Probably the worst thing she could have said to me at that moment."

Klaus and I were walking beside a body of water containing swans. In Europe one never knows if water is a lake, a canal, a river, a pond, or some other thing we don't have in North America. It was sunny out, as glorious as a 1968 *Come Visit Vienna!* pamphlet.

"Was the funeral the next day?"

"It was."

"What was that like?"

"A disaster."

"You're too hard on yourself."

"No, I mean it was literally a disaster. We thought it was only going to be maybe five or six people at the service—us, The Dwarf and an old girlfriend of Jeremy's, Jane. Yet when we arrived, there were about six other trashy-looking people already in the pews—three married couples, older, dressed in a way that seemed a bit . . . agricultural.

"We didn't know if they were Jeremy's foster parents or what, so we had to ask, which was awkward, and it turned out they *were* foster parents, and all I could do was stand there and hate them. I suppose the women were nice enough, and it was hard to imagine them being as grim as Jeremy had made them out to be, but the husbands were total jerks. I mean, these people *knew* each other.

"The men kept on talking and whispering throughout the service, and when we went to the cemetery, they continued talking, even while the minister was speaking. It was the end of December and the rain was pounding down like iron rods, and the dirt surrounding the casket was chocolate milk. My role in the service was to sing, so I did 'Amazing Grace' backwards. The guys snickered, so William asked them to be quiet, and they gave him louder, trashier snickering. William asked them again to be quiet, and they became huffy, like at closing time at a cocktail bar. Then one of the guys slipped and fell into the grave. He landed on his back."

"Gott!"

"It was really something. An ornament on the casket handle punctured his lung—you didn't have to be a genius to tell. Jane phoned 911, and the wife of the guy jumped into the hole along with Leslie. Leslie used to hand out Band-Aids for the ski team, so she got to play nurse, and she was shouting, 'Don't move him! If you do, then the handle will come out and let in dirt, his lung will collapse and he won't be able to breathe.' She was making things much worse.

"I'd stopped singing, of course, and the mud filled the grave's bottom like pig slops. It reminded me of the end of a horror movie when the dead emerge cackling from beneath the tombstones. William promptly landed in a fight with one of the two other guys, I don't even know what over. The buddy kept goading them on, so Mother went over to try to stop it, and as she approached them, she bumped into the buddy and he went into the grave too."

"Did your mother push him?"

"I'll never know."

"What happened next?"

"There were tears and . . . it was so ugly. Jeremy would have loved it."

"Did it go to the courts?"

"No. It was all just accident—rudeness and human stupidity."

"What happened after the funeral?"

"William and Leslie returned to their respective Disneyplaces, and I moved into Mother's."

"You couldn't go back to your apartment, could you?"

"No."

"That seems reasonable."

It was strange strolling through this slice of urban perfection, thinking about my little cube on the other end of the world. So many shop windows bursting with beauty and seduction and chocolates.

Klaus asked, "What then?"

"The Dwarf To Whom I Report gave me my job back, so I had my days filled. I was the office's official object of pity for a few weeks, but I soon lost that status. Donna had quit by then, so I didn't have to deal with her. It took me three months to be able to go back into my condo, and even then I had to go with William. He went in before me to turn on the lights, and then called me in."

"And?"

"I walked around, but I wouldn't touch anything. The

air was stale and too hot—the heat was on high and I never lowered it, I wanted to bake something bad from the rooms. I grabbed a few things I needed—pantyhose, blouses and cosmetics—and then bolted. William and I went there every day for weeks, until I was able to stay there the night and make peace with my fate. It took almost a year before going home stopped giving me the creeps. It's been six years since then."

* * *

What struck me with Klaus was how I went from one man in my life who'd lost his guiding visions to another suffering the same fate. "Klaus, you mean you'd never consider reverting to the man you were before this new OCD-controlling pill?"

Klaus seemed startled by the question. "Good God, no."

"Why not?" We were at our third meal. That's all people in Vienna seem to do—eat, and put in time between meals. That's not a complaint. I had some time on my hands to kill until Dr. Vogel forwarded all of the meteorite radiation data from Germany.

"Liz, I look at the man who I was even a month ago and I am depressed and sick to my soul."

Klaus was eating thymus glands (yes, sweetbreads) in a rooftop restaurant that was well concealed from anybody non-Austrian. It was a young and warm night, and the seating area was lit by hundreds of little white Christmas lights that covered the trees and the air above us.

Klaus said, "Because of my obsessive disorder, I never had a proper girlfriend, let alone a wife. Because of it, I never made long-lasting friendships. I feel like I'm starting my life over from the beginning."

"It can't be as extreme as all that."

He lowered his fork. "As of today, what do I have in my life?" He flashed me his winning smile. "Teeth. Thousands of teeth every day. The good thing about teeth is that they kept me sane. You've heard of people with Tourette's syndrome? Some of them become doctors and perform twelve-hour surgeries, but the moment they take off the gloves, the *fuck*s and *shit*s start right up. A man's life is thrown away because of too much or too little of some stupid molecule in his frontal cortex or his hypothalamus. Molecules. That's all it ever was—molecules."

I asked, "What was it you felt was so important to tell all these women in the street?"

"Those poor women. *Ach*—the embarrassment. I'd buy them all flowers and thank-you cards, but they'd take it the wrong way. They should all be allowed to boot me in the testicles. I deserve it."

"Klaus, be reasonable. You couldn't control yourself. Yes, you did all that crazy stuff, but at the same time it *wasn't* you."

"I accept no excuses."

"If I were you, I'd blame all those Freudian therapists who sucked in your money for all those years. I'm shocked that not once in all that time did they send you to a certified psychiatrist who could prescribe medications."

"Liz, Vienna has much history invested in Freudian—"

"Klaus, shut up. Just shut up." I was suddenly in a foul mood. Me, having dinner with the handsomest man in Europe at a chic rooftop restaurant, and I was in a foul mood. "You never said what it was that was so important that you had to badger all of those women."

Klaus's English had bad patches. "It was never an angry badgering that I did."

"What was it that was so important?"

He leaned back in his chair, and the eyes of everybody in the room were silently looking at him, as if his lovely face might yield a pearl. "I was always attracted to women who thought they were one hundred percent happy with the world, or what the world had to offer them. Not sexually attracted—morally attracted—though that sounds awful. I felt that I could make them aware of something far grander than what modern Vienna had to offer them."

"What would that be?"

"I no longer know."

Klaus was Jeremy's father in many ways. Their shared genetic strengths and weaknesses were fated to end at the same psychic cul-de-sac. I'd lost my appetite. My napkin dropped to the floor, but I didn't pick it up.

"Elizabeth, what has come over you?"

"Don't talk to me. Not right now."

"*Gott.* Have I lapsed and become compulsive in some way?"

"No, Klaus, you haven't." I was angry that I never got to witness him in his pre-paroxetine days—and I was angry because I know that if I had, I'd have seen the same Jeremy flash in the eyes, the same determination, the burning sun at the end of the highway, something that would make me willingly fall to my knees and crawl on pavement. He'd handed that role over to me, and nothing ever came of it. I felt cheated. I asked Klaus, "Have *you* ever had visions?"

"What do you mean, visions?"

"Visions. Have you seen things that were not real, but not dreams either—visions that showed you . . . I don't know—things humans have never seen before?"

"Maybe. Maybe not. But I would love to have done so."

"Jeremy saw visions."

Klaus raised his eyebrows.

"Yes, he did."

"What did he see?"

"Lots and little. I wrote down everything I could. It might have been poetry, or maybe it was merely his brain decaying, but I doubt it. The things he saw were always interesting to me. There was this one stream that started when I first met him, just before he became very sick."

"What was it?"

"He saw visions of farmers in the Prairies, wheat farmers. It was spring, but they weren't planting their fields."

"Go on."

"These farmers believed that the world was going to end that winter, so they didn't bother sowing their grain. I think they set fire to their seeds. The farmers believed it was the end of time. Their wives and children were on the porches of their houses, and they were throwing away all of the jarred preserves and dried foods they'd made the year before."

"And?"

"A voice came down from the sky. It told them that the world could only ever be full of sorrow, and that calamity and disaster will happen, always, either by their own deeds or by God's choice. That's why they shouldn't be afraid—because the end is going to happen no matter what." I stopped and took notice of how cheerful the rooftop restaurant looked, each of its tiny white lights tinkling my brain like a child's xylophone. The restaurant was the opposite of how I felt. I said, "Klaus, I've thought about Jeremy's visions many times now. I know them by heart."

He said nothing, so I continued.

"The farmers heard a woman's voice from the sky, telling them there was a gift awaiting them. They were told they would soon be given a signal—and that they'd soon receive this gift. But then the voice said that the farmers were unable to tell the difference between being awake and being asleep. She told them they'd lost their belief in the possibility of change. She said that death without the possibility of changing the world was the same as a life that never was. The farmers and their wives and their families were told that they weren't going to be receiving their gift—not that year. But by then it was too late to plant seeds. Their stored foods had been destroyed. They knew winter would arrive, and they had no idea what came next."

Klaus's listening was intense, almost aggressive.

I continued. "So the farmers stood on the road, a dirt road covered in dust. They stood there and prayed for a sign that would tell them they hadn't been abandoned."

"And?"

"A big string came down from the sky, as if dangled from outer space. There was a human bone hanging at the end. The farmers then saw another string lower to earth, and it had a skull tied to its end. Then there were more and more strings—hundreds of bones that all clattered like wind chimes. The farmers knew they'd received their message. They were forsaken, and they were in the wilderness. They felt that they weren't even human any more, just scarecrows or showroom mannequins, stripped of souls. Their only salvation lay in placing faith in the very entity who had forsaken them."

"And?"

"And that's where that vision ended. That was his biggest story, but he never finished it."

"My son was a mystic, then."

"You might say so."

Music was playing—Strauss. It sounded like music from a thousand years ago.

Klaus looked at me and said, "I am the same as our son. I can see that. He and I both reached the same point before we stopped. Hit the wall, as I think you say."

I was crying.

"I'm sorry, Liz."

"Why is life never what you want it to be?" I was tired. I wanted to go home, but home wasn't home any more. I could no more live in my condo again than on Mars. It was a box, just a box.

The waiter came and asked us if we wanted dessert. We passed. Klaus sat there looking at the tabletop, shiny, reflecting all those pretty little white lights. And here's where I made a leap. I said, "Klaus—"

He said, "Yes," but didn't look up at me.

I placed my hand on the table in front of him. I said, "Klaus, you're lonely too, aren't you?"

Again he said, "Yes." He took my hand in both of his, kissed it. He looked in my eyes, and that's when we fell in love. He knew, and I knew. It changed nothing, and yet it changed everything. *So this is what everybody's been talking about.*

* * *

The world is a strange place. I'm flying above it right now, in a 777, with Klaus. I suspect this journal is coming to an end—or at least the end has arrived for the Liz Dunn who used to be, the Liz Dunn who was too lonely to live, and too frightened to die.

We're flying to Vancouver to stay in a hotel for a week while we throw away everything I own and sell my condo to the first person who bites. I'm trying to think of anything I want to keep, but come up blank. Perhaps one of Jeremy's leftover prescription bottles now filled with dust. Some photos. His scraps of paper with words written on them.

Here's something: Klaus has never flown before—imagine that! I'm allowed to witness someone seeing the world for the first time. What a rare treat.

It's been a busy three months for me. Klaus got the information from the German government, detailing the amount and types of radiation I'd been exposed to. I'm afraid to say it wasn't good news, but I was flattered by Klaus's anger at God. I told him, "Look, Klaus, just let it go. I'm not angry—so don't you be angry." But of course he stews, yet I'm quite serene about it all. I have headaches and I vomit every so often, but I'm also pregnant—surprise!—so in my head and my body there's this race between life and death going on. But then isn't that the case for everybody who's ever lived, forever and always? Isn't that the nature of being alive?

Klaus has a window seat. The captain says we're over the Orkney Islands right now—what a funny name, the Orkneys—like the name of problem neighbours who have too many Rottweilers. Like a child, Klaus has just pointed out to me another jet off in the distance: *Two jets in the air at once!* To think that all this cosmopolitan grown man ever had to do to see the world was simply to go and buy a ticket.

* * *

A few weeks ago, on the same day I confirmed my pregnancy, I had a headache so big it seemed like it could change the weather. I was screaming for something, anything, to make it go away, so Klaus gave me a snack from his dental lunch box that he assured me wouldn't hurt the baby. It killed the pain, but it did something else to me too. Suddenly I was in the Prairies, and I was with the forsaken farmers who were watching as giant wind chimes made of bones tinkled and clattered in a breeze no bigger than a child's whisper.

And then I was up above the farmers—I was above the Prairies, and I was looking at them and their wives and children, and then I realized that I was the voice speaking down from the sky.

I said to them, "People, you're now in the wilderness. You have a choice before you, and you have a winter of cold and starvation during which to make that choice."

They asked me, "What is our choice?"

And I said, "You have to decide whether you want God to be here with you as a part of your everyday life, or whether you want God to be distant from you, not returning until you've created a world perfect enough for Him to re-enter."

"That is our choice?"

And I said, "That's it."

I snapped my fingers, and with that the bones and strings fell from the sky, making cones of thread on the road and in the stubbled fields. When I came to, my head felt like a room with all the windows open, letting in gusts of cool fresh air.

* * *

The captain tells us we're just about to pass over Reykjavik, and so I think this is where things really do end, and what's so wrong with things ending? It's kind of nice not to know for sure what happens to us before we're born or after we die—or to be unsure of what will happen to us in that nervous, iffy time that exists between the point at which we decide to change our lives and the point where our lives actually change.

Klaus just tugged my sleeve and pointed out some stars above Iceland, visible in the day. Will wonders never cease? I look at those stars and I pluck them from the sky, and flick them at you like diamonds, like seeds.

You are the everything, and everything is in you.

Goodbye, all of you.

Your friend,

Liz.

A Note on the Author

Douglas Coupland is a novelist who also works in visual arts and theater. His novels include *Generation X*, *All Families Are Psychotic*, and *Hey Nostradamus!* He lives and works in Vancouver, Canada. For more information, visit www.coupland.com.